"My father told me to be kind to you."

Miranda swallowed hard, refusing to meet Quint's eyes.

"And now I see why," he went on. "Well, the kindest thing I can tell you, Miranda, is that I think your family treats you unfairly. They're as responsible for this whole mess as you."

"What?" Miranda stared at him in surprise.

He remained standing over her sternly. "I said they're responsible, too. It doesn't sound as if they ever gave you any guidance or affection. Now you're in trouble and they send you away—ignore you. Families are supposed to *love* each other, Miranda."

Quint's words hurt—but she knew they were true. She'd always been the family outcast. But she was amazed to hear him use a word as emotional as love. Hearing it from his lips made her feel dizzy with yearning, knowing his affection was only temporary.

Bethany Campbell, an English major, teacher and textbook consultant, calls her writing world her "hidey-hole," that marvelous place where true love always wins out. Her hobbies include writing poetry and thinking about that little scar on Harrison Ford's chin. She laughingly admits that her husband, who produces videos and writes comedy, approves of the first one only.

Books by Bethany Campbell

Flirtation River
Bethany Campbell

Harlequin Books

TORONTO • NEW YORK • LONDON
AMSTERDAM • PARIS • SYDNEY • HAMBURG
STOCKHOLM • ATHENS • TOKYO • MILAN

ISBN 0-373-02911-X

Harlequin Romance first edition June 1988

To Lucy Babcock

CHAPTER ONE

"I DON'T KNOW what to say," said the Senator, shaking his head angrily.

Miranda knew this meant he was going to say a great deal, most of it unpleasant, and she tried to look both cheerful and brave. She felt neither.

"Father," Jaqueline said softly. "Don't upset yourself. I'm sure Miranda will try to be reasonable. Won't you, dear? You'll *try*, won't you?"

Miranda looked gratefully at her elder sister. Then her eyes traveled back to her father, the Senator. He was a tall, dignified, dark-eyed man, and he sat behind his desk with his hands tightly clenched on its walnut surface. His face was set in an expression of cold fury.

Jaqueline, a small, frailer version of their father, sat in a chair at his right. Her hands, too, were clenched, but in her lap, in a distressed and ladylike way. Miranda had the uncomfortable feeling she was before a firing squad.

Whenever Miranda was summoned to the study of her father's Georgetown mansion, she knew she was in trouble. That day was no exception. Her father was red-faced and dangerously on edge. Jaqueline had a look of pained sweetness and patience. It was an expression she often wore in Miranda's presence.

The Senator stood. He began to pace. He strode past photographs of himself as a handsome diplomatic attaché, an imposing ambassador and, finally, a distinguished congressman. There were also pictures of Jaqueline, from the time she was a small and ladylike child. There were no pictures at all of Miranda.

The Senator glowered at Miranda. "I don't know what you did to bring this on," he said, waving a typewritten letter in the air as if it were a flag of battle. "But this time you've gone too far, Miranda. When, young lady, are you going to get some sense into your head?"

Jaqueline sighed deeply. "Father, you have to realize Miranda doesn't understand the significance of these letters." She smiled with sorrowful forebearance. "If you won't help yourself, Miranda, we'll have to do it for you. And please understand, Father *is* doing his best."

Jaqueline sighed again. She was pale, delicate and sat with the strictest propriety. She always managed to look saintlike.

Miranda scrunched down in her Queen Anne chair. She was tall and curvaceous, with a golden tan and streaked honey-blond hair that hung just below her shoulders. Compared with Jaqueline, she looked scandalously healthy and anything but saintly. She had full lips, lovely cheekbones and a pert nose that gave her an air of mischief. Her eyes were long-lashed and gray green, tilted like a kitten's. Right now, her gaze was downcast so she wouldn't see the Senator's rage.

"Just what have you got yourself into this time?" the Senator fumed, waving the letter under Miranda's nose.

"I don't know," Miranda answered unhappily. "At first I thought they were just—a bad joke."

"Joke?" her father said sharply. "It's disgusting. This— this person keeps writing and telling you to get out of the country—or else. I knew one day you'd push one of those wild boys too far. And now you have."

Miranda leaned her chin on her fist miserably. "Daddy," she said as reasonably as she could, "it might be somebody I don't even know. I haven't done anything to make anybody write these things—honest."

Her father made a sound of disgruntlement. "Don't try to placate me, Miranda. You brought this on yourself, and you know it. Wasn't it just last year that young man tried to commit suicide over you?"

"*Poor* Miranda," Jaqueline breathed, and clasped her hands together more tightly.

Miranda pressed her chin against her fist more stubbornly. "That whole thing was blown all out of proportion."

"A boy throws himself out of a window over you, and you say it was blown out of proportion? No wonder you get yourself into these scrapes." The Senator shook his head in disgust.

"Daddy," Miranda protested with honest indignation, "all I did was tell him I didn't want to go out with him again. He went back to the fraternity house and started drinking. He kept calling me up and telling me if I didn't change my mind, he'd jump out the window. I knew he was being silly, so I told him to go ahead."

"A typically irresponsible act," accused the Senator. "You drove him to desperation, then told him to jump out a window."

"Daddy! The fraternity house had only one story. I could see him from my dorm window. I knew he had other boys there, egging him on. So what if he jumped? All he did was land in a rosebush and get scratched."

"And you dragged the family name into every cheap tabloid in the country. 'Senator Mason's Daughter Drives Football Hero to Suicide Attempt.' Do you care nothing for my work? My reputation?"

"Of course she does," soothed Jaqueline. "She just forgets." She turned her patient gaze to Miranda. "You have to control your impulsiveness, dear. You have to remember Father's position."

"I try," Miranda defended herself. "It's just—well, things keep happening. Now it's these letters. I mean, Daddy, if you think this letter writer is dangerous, shouldn't you call the police?"

"You've probably driven him over the edge," Senator Mason said darkly. "And no, I don't want the police involved. I don't want any more publicity about you, young lady, especially this type of thing. You've put me through enough."

Miranda looked away from him guiltily. He was as tall and handsome as ever, but his face was florid with anger.

"These letters aren't exactly fun for me, either," she murmured.

"Fun, unfortunately, is all you've ever thought about for twenty-one years," he snarled. "And the more poorly it reflects on me, the more fun you seem to find it."

"That's not true," Miranda objected, sinking lower into her chair.

"It is true," her father contradicted. "It's been true from the time you were a child. Do you remember when I made the mistake of taking you to meet the high lama of Cambasia?"

"Oh," Jaqueline said faintly, "that was so embarrassing."

Miranda remembered the incident all too clearly. It was the first time she'd made the headlines. Her father had been ambassador to Cambasia. She was four and Jaqueline was eight. The high lama, the most important and revered holy man in Cambasia, had granted her father an audience and expressly asked him to bring his two daughters.

For a week and a half the household drilled Miranda on how to act in the holy man's august presence. But when he appeared, all the training flew from her childish mind. She looked at the aged man with delight, especially taken by his beautiful long saffron robe.

The robe enchanted her so much she forgot all protocol. "Hey!" she had piped, stepping up to him and holding out her skirt proudly. "You and me both got yellow dresses! But my panties are white. And got lace. Do yours?" Then she triumphantly lifted her skirt to show him the lace edging her underwear.

The lama had laughed and laughed, but Miranda's father was livid. Jaqueline had cried softly all the way home. "Miranda showed a holy man her pants!" she wept in humiliation. The press loved it, but Miranda had to eat alone in her room for the next two weeks as punishment.

"Remember when you were nine?" the Senator asked with ill-humored derision. "And you and the prince of Kangastan pushed the royal adviser into his own swimming pool? You disrupted this country's relationship with Kangastan for a full week."

Glumly Miranda remembered. The prince had been ten and full of the royal devil. He and Miranda had hit it off splendidly.

"I'd told you and told you," Jaqueline said mournfully. "One is never to touch the person of anyone of the court of Kangastan."

"Well, it was the prince's idea," Miranda protested, color flooding her cheeks. "I thought since he was the prince, it'd be all right."

"All right," mocked the Senator. "I suppose you thought it was all right when you sold kisses at a college fair to raise money for the Save the Small Farmer movement?"

Miranda chanced a peep at Jaqueline, who was shaking her head sadly.

"Some of the boys involved asked me," Miranda said defensively. "They said I could raise a lot of money for them."

"And you did," the Senator exploded. "Conveniently forgetting those radicals have opposed my farm policies for years. They are my political enemies."

"I thought it would show I was open-minded," Miranda murmured miserably.

"It showed you were empty-minded. They were using you to undermine my credibility. All you saw was another chance to flaunt yourself. You had no business mixing with those people. They are my foes."

"I didn't think that anyone would make such a fuss—" Miranda began to explain.

"You don't *think*, period," the Senator snapped. "You were eighteen years old. You should have known better."

"The problem," Jaqueline pointed out gently, "is you shouldn't try to think for yourself, Miranda. There are people we mix with and people we don't. Your emotions always get in the way. You must try to see the bigger picture—in terms of Father's mission."

Miranda felt dangerously close to tears. She needed help with present problems, not a recounting of past sins.

"That's all ancient history," she pleaded. "What about these letters? If you think this is some maniac, are you just going to let him stalk me?"

"Miranda," the Senator admonished severely, "spare the melodrama. I am, of course, concerned for your welfare."

"Father," Jaqueline put in, her voice quavering, "what worries me is that someone is using Miranda to get to you. You might be in jeopardy yourself. That's what disturbs me most—the effect of all this on you."

The Senator regarded Miranda gravely. "If there's a possibility of real danger, it could touch Jaqueline, as well. You, as usual, see no farther than yourself. You have a talent for creating trouble, Miranda. I don't know how much you've stirred up this time, but, yes, I intend to do something."

"Yes," Jaqueline said, nodding resignedly. "Father's decided to take action."

Miranda looked at them. "What?" she asked with trepidation.

"First," her father scowled, "I'm going to hire a detective to discreetly investigate this mess—and see whom you've driven to distraction. Second, I'm doing precisely as those letters advise. I'm sending you away."

"Away?" wailed Miranda. "But I haven't even been home two weeks—I haven't met Jaqueline's new boyfriend yet. I want to meet him! And I've been good—I did well at this last college, Daddy. I passed everything."

"Yes," he replied sourly. "But you got three C minus grades. Not good enough, young lady. Besides that, you managed to get into this atrocious business with these letters. Next fall I'm sending you somewhere else."

Miranda blinked hard and tried to keep her chin from quivering. She could never follow Jaqueline's example and earn A's in all her courses. She'd never had her sister's passion for being best. Besides, Miranda was never in one place long enough to get used to an academic schedule. Her father kept making her change schools in hopes her grades would undergo a miraculous cure. They never did, and she felt like an eternal failure.

"Perhaps there's someplace you can do better," Jaqueline said with an optimistic smile.

"And next time," Senator Mason practically bellowed, "I want you to behave yourself. Stop getting your picture in the paper. Stop trying to conquer every man on campus.

And stop bringing incidents like this—'' he brandished the letter ''—down on your head. Sometimes I think you lie awake nights thinking up these stunts.''

Miranda could make no reply. She knew it would be useless. Her picture got into the paper because she was the Senator's daughter and she was lively and photogenic. She had been born with a kind of natural gaiety that sprang more from an overabundance of energy than actual wildness. Lately that gaiety was swiftly dwindling.

She didn't try to conquer every man on campus. The past year, ever since the notorious "suicide attempt," she had dated little, trying to tone down her excesses of enthusiasm. It had only made people think she was aloof. Now her own family didn't want her around. She felt as lost and lonely as if she lived in outer space.

"I said I was sending you away, and I am. For your own good—and my blood pressure."

"I worry about your blood pressure, Father," Jaqueline said solicitously. "But try to understand Miranda's just been slow to mature. It's hard for her to understand the issues at stake. You mustn't let it affect your health. You're too important to the country."

The Senator simply shook his head. He looked at the letter, then at Miranda. "I don't understand how you get into these things. I don't understand you."

By sheer willpower she forced back the tears that threatened. She set her jaw at a jaunty angle. "Well," she said, as flippantly as she could, "I don't mind getting out of Washington. Nobody ever talks anything but politics. I hope you picked someplace interesting for me. England would be nice. Or Paris would be lovely."

"Good." An almost malicious satisfaction throbbed in the Senator's voice. "Because it's not too far from England. And not much farther from Paris."

Miranda frowned slightly. Geography was not her strong point. She tried to hide her perplexity behind bravado. "Where?" she asked. "Belgium?" Belgium had been pleasant. She had spent a semester at school there.

"It's not far from England, Arkansas, and it's not far from Paris, Texas," he said with that same, almost vengeful satisfaction. "It's a little town called Cherry Creek, Arkansas. I'm sending you to stay with an ex-marine sergeant who used to work for us back in our days with the Cambasian Embassy. Duke Wilcox. He's an iron-bottomed old disciplinarian. He can keep you in line—and knock the socks off anybody who tries to come after you. He's a retired truck driver or something now. He's got a housekeeper who can serve as chaperon. And you, young lady, will behave as if she's an army of chaperons—I don't want any more scandal."

Miranda sat through this vitriolic speech with an expression of sheer horror. She remembered Duke Wilcox quite clearly. Cambasia was a trouble spot, and Duke Wilcox was assigned to the Mason family as special private guard. He had a face like a bulldog, a voice like the boom of thunder and hair as red as a forest fire.

Her father had forbidden her and Jaqueline to play with Cambasian children; he didn't want his daughters mingling with the natives. But Miranda, the misfit even then, liked the gardener's two shy and giggling sons. Repeatedly she slipped away to play with them. Repeatedly Duke Wilcox caught her. He would pounce on her with a nerve-shattering cry, snatch her up and carry her back to the house, yelling all the way that she had to mind her daddy. He had terrified her.

Now she was going to be living under his bloodshot eye in a place she'd never heard of. Great, she thought. Just great. He could tell her truck-driving stories, show her his tattoos and open beer bottles with his teeth.

"Duke Wilcox?" she asked weakly.

Jaqueline sighed sympathetically. "I'm sorry, Miranda. I thought you'd be better out of the country. Monte Carlo or someplace, with lots of young men to keep you busy."

"I don't want to think of what kind of trouble Miranda could get into in Monte Carlo," growled the Senator. "Run off with a race-car driver or a beach bum."

"But if that's what makes her happy," Jaqueline said with a resigned philosophical expression. "I've tried to be both mother and sister to Miranda. But sometimes I wonder if we should try to keep forcing her into our own mold when she just won't fit . . . I just don't know."

"My mind is made up," the Senator said flatly.

"I don't think Cherry Creek is a very good idea, Daddy," Miranda offered tentatively. She raised her gray-green eyes to his cold brown ones. "We should talk this over some more. And maybe you should discuss it with Buford—or somebody."

Buford, she thought with desperation—he would help her. In the whole household it was only Buford, the butler, she could count as an ally. Jaqueline was too sweet actually to take sides against Miranda. But Jaqueline also agreed with everything their father ever said or was likely to say. Buford was her only hope. He'd worked for her father as long as she could remember. The Senator had a surprising respect for Buford's opinions—sometimes.

"I've already talked to Buford." A cool smile frosted the Senator's lips.

Jaqueline nodded pensively. "It was Buford's idea to send you to Cherry Creek. He even arranged it. I want you to know *I* was against it, Miranda. I knew you wouldn't be happy there." She sighed.

"Buford? He arranged it?" Miranda asked in disbelief.

"Buford and Wilcox were friends back in the Cambasian days," the Senator pronounced. "They've kept in touch. I'd almost forgotten about Wilcox until Buford mentioned his name. And Wilcox could handle you then, and he can handle you now."

So Buford had betrayed her, Miranda thought, sparks starting to light her eyes. Some friend. Some ally. Was there no one she could trust? She'd find him later and tell him exactly what she thought.

"One more thing," her father added. "Buford says Wilcox has two sons. Stay away from them. You've always had an unfortunate tendency to mix with rabble."

"You're overly gregarious, Miranda," Jaqueline said. "And you see, now it's got you into trouble again. I'm so sorry you have to go through this."

Miranda wriggled uncomfortably in her chair. Then she remembered the Senator hated wriggling and went as still as she could.

"You'll stay in Cherry Creek until this thing is resolved," the Senator said grumpily. "And you're going to behave—or Duke Wilcox has my permission to use any means to bring you back into line. Stay away from his sons and any other inappropriate locals." Her father turned his back to her with an air that told her she was dismissed. Jaqueline sat staring down at her pale fingers as if mourning the confusion that had descended upon the household, thanks to Miranda.

Miranda's feelings were hurt, but she'd grown used to that. Lately her father acted as if he were within a hair's breadth of disowning her.

She rose, resolving to confront Buford. The Senator turned and glanced at her without affection. He handed her the letter. "Here," he said acidly. "Don't forget your fan mail."

She looked down at the folded page, trying to keep emotion from showing in her face. She knew the letter's each sinister word by heart:

Dear Miss Glamor Girl, Miss Tease, Miss Hot Stuff,
Get out of this countree and stay out because if you
don't get out of hear maybe somethin will happin to
make you not so pretty. I am watching you Miranda
and I don't like what I see. Go away and stay away or I
don't know what I mite do.

                                                    The Watcher

She took the letter silently, trying to appear unashamed. Her father had always been cool to her, but since her twenty-first birthday he had been positively glacial. She felt a genuine physical ache within, a pain in her midsection, but she ignored it just as she always did.

Jaqueline glanced up at her with dark, tragic eyes. "I'm sorry," she mouthed, then smiled in demure encouragement.

Miranda tried to smile back but couldn't. She rose, squared her shoulders and left the room.

Once outside the study, she felt stronger, her old spirit returning. She thought of Buford's treachery and set out to track him down. She found him in the dining room, checking to see which silver needed polishing. She stalked into the room with what she hoped was impressive indignation.

"You!" she said to Buford, shooting him a look of betrayed resentment.

"And you," Buford replied with perfect calm, glancing first at her, then back at the sterling condiment set. He seemed to find the silver far more interesting.

"You're the one responsible for this, Buford," she accused. "Daddy's sending me to that vile Wilcox man in Cherry Creek—wherever that is—and he told me it was your idea. How could you?" Her gray-green eyes flashed fire. She drew herself up to her full height—five feet, seven inches. She folded her arms imperiously.

Buford was not daunted. He was a tall black man of tightly controlled dignity. "Seems you have somebody after you, Miranda," he said matter-of-factly. "Well, he won't find you in Cherry Creek. And if he does, Duke Wilcox can protect you. The man's as good as a whole battalion of marines."

"I don't want to go," she said stubbornly. "Talk to Daddy again. I won't go."

"Appears to me," Buford said, his dark eyes appraising her sardonically, "that you don't have much choice. That you have landed yourself in a heap of trouble. That you just might have yourself flat out in danger this time."

He spoke with such calm conviction that Miranda suddenly knew it was useless to argue. Well, she thought, deflated, Buford wouldn't back down, and her anger didn't faze him. She tried a different tack. "Just why," she asked, her arms still crossed, "does everybody think I caused this? Why is it my fault? It's like some judge and jury already tried me and found me guilty."

"I would say," Buford offered dryly, "that it's your track record. Up to the time you were twelve, you were the worst tomboy I ever did see. Then all of a sudden, boom! You get transformed by puberty, and you become the worst flirt I ever did see. Not a bad girl, mind you, just a flirty one. As if you don't know a girl like you don't ever have to flirt. Still, you are not what I myself would call an inhibited personality."

Miranda sighed, unfolded her arms and thrust her hands deeply into the pockets of her fashionably crinkled linen slacks. "Buford," she said wearily, "you've already made my day hard enough. Don't psychoanalyze me." Buford took night courses in psychology and had the irritating habit of analyzing everyone's character and motives.

"I don't have to psychoanalyze you," Buford said with a superior glance. "You're too easy to figure out. You want attention. You don't get any here, so you just go out and grab it someplace else. You're good at it. This time, unfortunately, you were a little too good. So I think you better stop protesting and aim on spending time in Cherry Creek."

"Rats," said Miranda, tossing her gold-streaked hair. She hated it when Buford talked this way. Too often he was exactly right. "I don't try to get attention," she said, attempting to undermine his argument. "Not anymore. For a long time I was always the new person in school—I wanted to fit in, and I guess I tried too hard. But I've stopped doing that."

Buford examined the luster on a pair of candlesticks, found it wanting and set them aside for the maid to polish. "Well, when you did it, you did it with a vengeance," he observed. "Remember your freshman year, when you went to the fraternity party in that leopard-skin costume? And somehow a picture of you dancing on a table got into *People* magazine with the caption 'Senator's Daughter Party Animal' under it? Your daddy was humiliated. And this letter business is the last straw. The way I see it, we've got to protect you from yourself. And if you have changed, you just go to Cherry Creek and prove it."

Miranda wrinkled her nose. She pulled out a chair and straddled it, facing its back. Buford gave her a look that told her a proper lady didn't sit on a chair in such a way. She gave him a look that told him she didn't care.

"If anybody else wore a fake leopard skin and danced on a table, it would just be chalked up to high spirits or something. It wasn't that horrible."

"The problem is," Buford said piously, "that you are not anybody else. You're the daughter of a senator. You have got to behave. You have got to set an example. Like Miss Jaqueline keeps telling you," he added slyly.

Miranda blushed. She settled her chin on the back of the chair and watched Buford examine the Senator's silver goblets. She had never been the slightest bit like Jaqueline and never could be.

"I'll never measure up to her," she said, resigned. "You forget—Jaqueline's perfect. I'm not."

Buford lightly buffed a silver ice bucket and put it back in the cabinet. He turned and gave her a teasing look. For the first time, he smiled. Buford had a wonderful smile, and it always warmed her. It seemed to say, "You're a scamp, a rascal and a rapscallion, but I like you."

What he actually said, however, was "One thing I never forget, Miranda, is that you're not perfect. Oh my, no. That is just about impossible to forget."

Miranda made a silly face at him and stuck out her tongue. He glanced around to make sure nobody was watching. Then he made a worse face and stuck out his own tongue.

They looked at each other, then both laughed. She loved Buford, even though he had helped engineer her coming exile. He could be just as stern as her father, but she felt he really cared about her, and he was never cold. Why couldn't her father be more like him?

She knew why. She had been told. Twenty-five years ago, Jaqueline had been born. Doctors advised her mother not to have another baby. But Jaqueline was such a lovely child, so delicate and possessing a natural politeness, that her mother had tried to have one more flawless offspring. Instead, twenty-one years ago she bore Miranda and died.

Jaqueline had been so shaken by the loss of their mother that she developed health problems: asthma, lack of endurance, difficulty keeping on weight. Jaqueline never complained, but Miranda blamed herself and felt her father did, too.

The feeling of warmth Miranda had shared with Buford faded. She grew sober. She had tried hard to please her father. She tried hard to live up to Jaqueline's high standards. But she never could.

Buford understood. He came to her chair, put his big hand on her shoulder and gave it a squeeze. "Do you good to get away, Miranda," he said. "Your daddy's been a hard man to please lately. Like I say—go. Prove yourself. Duke Wilcox, he's rough on the outside but good deep down."

He gave her shoulder another affectionate squeeze, then, embarrassed, turned his attention back to the silver. Privately he'd never quite believed the story about Mrs. Mason wanting another little Jaqueline. Jaqueline was so much like the Senator it was as if two versions of the same person were living in the house. He secretly theorized that Miranda's mother, in self-defense, had wanted a child with more individuality, more character, not a miniature cold-blooded diplomat programmed by the state department. But he kept his opinions to himself.

"I haven't even met Jaqueline's new boyfriend," Miranda mused mournfully.

"You ain't missed much," Buford replied with a sniff. "He's off on some state-department business all this month."

"She sounds serious this time," Miranda sighed. "Do you think she'll marry him?"

"If her main criterion is dullness," Buford replied, "I believe she's found her man."

Miranda blinked at him in surprise but said nothing. She sat, resting her chin on the back of the chair. At last she spoke. "Daddy says Duke Wilcox is a retired truck driver," she said moodily. "That doesn't sound like the essence of excitement, either."

"Your daddy said that?" Buford queried mildly. "Hmmph."

Miranda watched him inspect the grape shears. "Yes. Is that what he is?"

Buford gave an elaborate shrug. He smiled innocently. "I don't believe he's retired. But he does work with trucks. Yes, indeedy. Fine machine, the truck. Backbone of U.S. transportation."

Miranda was not impressed. She just became more depressed. Jaqueline appeared in the doorway. "Miranda," she said in her sweetly controlled voice, "I'd like to talk to you a moment. Alone. Would you step out, Buford? Immediately, please?"

Buford nodded politely. "Consider me stepped out," he replied smoothly. He glided away as silently as a ghost.

Jaqueline came up behind Miranda and put her hands on her sister's shoulders. "I want you to know," she said, performing a stiff little massage on Miranda's tense muscles, "that I did my best to keep Father from sending you to Cherry Creek. I know there are places you'd be happier. Why don't you go out and cheer yourself up by going shopping, dear?"

"I don't feel like shopping," Miranda replied gloomily. "All I ever do when I'm home is shop."

Jaqueline leaned over and pecked her dryly on the cheek. "But it's something you're good at," she soothed. "I think you help Father win a few votes from the fashion-conscious.

You know I don't have time for that kind of thing. Besides, I find it frivolous. But it amuses you. Run along and buy yourself some new things for Cherry Creek."

"And just what," Miranda asked bleakly, "does one wear in Cherry Creek? Overalls? Combat boots?"

"Something casual and elegant, but not sporty. You know how Father hates sporty-looking women," Jaqueline advised. "After all, you still represent Father—even in Cherry Creek. I'm sure the people down there are starved to see real fashion. It's a little thing you can do for Father."

Miranda nodded without enthusiasm. All through college she'd tried to soothe herself with beautiful clothes. She probably had too many. It seemed ostentatious. But Jaqueline was right: shopping seemed the only thing for which Miranda showed the least talent. That—and getting into trouble.

CHAPTER TWO

THE DAY BEFORE Miranda was to fly from Washington to Arkansas, Duke Wilcox climbed under the jacked-up cab of a diesel truck. Duke was not, as the Senator thought, a retired trucker but the owner and president of the largest truckline in the Southwest. He was also as bullheaded and bossy as ever and was going to show the blankety-blank mechanic exactly how a brake line should be fixed.

Duke Wilcox was not simply a big man, he was huge. When he rolled under the truck on his dolly, he accidentally kicked the jack. The truck came down, and the weight of the heavy tire fractured his left leg.

The break was so critical the doctor had Duke flown to the Little Rock Veterans' Hospital. His household and family erupted into such turmoil that everyone forgot that Miranda was coming.

It was Duke's younger son, Jerry, who finally remembered. Jerry was tired, worried and drinking what seemed to be his sixteenth cup of bitter hospital coffee when he remembered about Miranda. He swore.

Quint, his older brother, leaned against a pillar. He had managed about two hours of sleep the night before in the waiting room. Every time Quint dozed off, Mrs. Petitjean, Duke's housekeeper, would start crying. Quint had comforted her as best he could. She was a rather hysterical woman, and even though doctors assured them that Duke would be fine, she kept breaking into great, racking sobs about how Mr. Wilcox could have been killed.

"What's wrong?" Quint asked Jerry. He cast a weary glance at Mrs. Petitjean. He hoped she wasn't about to cry again.

"The damned girl—" Jerry said, smacking his forehead. "I just remembered. That stupid Senator's daughter—she's coming in—"

"Oh, no!" wailed Mrs. Petitjean, bursting into tears. "I didn't want him to get involved with them in the first place! Somebody's threatening that girl. It's probably dangerous to even have her around. I can't have her in the house all by myself! I'm a defenseless woman! I couldn't protect myself—let alone her!"

Mrs. Petitjean began to boohoo so loudly that Quint was forced to pat her shoulder. "No problem," he said to his brother. "We phone Washington, explain the circumstances and tell her not to come."

"We can't," Jerry grumbled, staring up from the plastic-upholstered couch. He looked exactly like his father, strong-jawed, massively built, with hair the color of flame.

"Yes, we can," Quint said grimly. "To hell with the Senator, and to hell with his daughter. Pop's had a bad accident. We have to change our plans."

"I can't be expected to take care of her," wailed Mrs. Petitjean. "I'd be a nervous wreck having someone in the house who's marked for violence!"

Quint gave her another mechanical pat. "You won't have to, Mrs. Petitjean," he said. "We'll tell her not to come."

He leaned against the pillar again. He was thirty-two and did not resemble his father or brother in the slightest. He had their height but none of their bulk. He was whipcord lean everywhere except in the breadth of his shoulders. His hair was thick, straight and the dark, shining brown of polished walnut. He had high cheekbones, so prominent that there were hollows beneath them. With his aquiline nose and the chiseled sweep of his jawline, he looked like a man born not for this century but the one before. His was a totally Western face and looked as if it had been designed for a Texas Ranger or the sheriff of Tombstone, Arizona. He did not look like the kind of man interested in running a business, and he was not. He had his own pursuits.

Jerry raked a hand through his red hair. He was the son who would eventually run Deerfield Trucking full-time. "I can't tell her not to come," he said sarcastically. "It's a little late. She's due at the airport in an hour."

Quint glanced at his watch. This time he swore. Mrs. Petitjean still blubbered, which made his head hurt. "We'll send her back," he said shortly. His eyes were a darker blue than his brother's, deeply set and thickly lashed. They could look surprisingly gentle or impressively cold. At the moment they were so cold they were polar. He nodded curtly in Mrs. Petitjean's direction. "Emma can't handle it," he said quietly. "That's obvious."

"Yeah?" Jerry asked, rubbing his freckled brow irritably. "Think about this. As soon as Pop wakes up, he's going to want to know where the Senator's daughter is. And if you send her back, he'll raise the roof. You know how Pop feels about breaking a promise. One of us is going to have to take her."

"Go ahead!" Quint protested, standing straighter, rebellion flashing in the dark blue eyes. "She's all yours."

"Wrong," Jerry countered. "Have you ever seen this woman's picture?"

Quint didn't respond. He'd seen pictures all right. His father kept a scrapbook on the exploits of Senator Mason. This puzzled Quint, because he suspected his father couldn't stand the Senator. Duke seemed delighted whenever the

Senator's daughter got into a scrape. He practically crowed
when he'd shown Quint the famous "party animal" picture. "Ha!" Duke Wilcox had snorted. "She'll keep the old
boy spinning. Look at her! She ain't one he'll beat into the
ground—I guarantee you."

Quint had to admit that Miranda looked splendid in
leopard skin.

But she wasn't his type. He didn't like blondes, he especially didn't like flashy blondes, and he didn't like tall
women. He liked them petite, understated, with an air of
vulnerability.

Jerry watched him, exasperation on his ruddy face. "I
said, have you ever seen this girl's picture?"

"I've seen her picture," Quint said moodily. "She looks
like trouble."

"Right," Jerry said, nodding vociferously. "And remember me? I'm getting married in three months. You
think Annette would tolerate having that blonde move in
with me? Think again. No. Pop wants the girl taken care of.
And you're the one who's gonna have to do it."

Quint drew up to his full height. Cold determination
flashed deep in his eyes. "No," he said simply.

"She'll be safer at your place anyway," Jerry insisted,
conviction growing. "I can't put her up. Pop's out of com-
mission and Emma can't handle her alone. You're the only
choice. Your place on the river's perfect. She'll be so far
back in the woods, nobody'll ever find her."

"No," Quint repeated firmly.

"She'll be away from everybody up there. It's perfect,"
Jerry said persuasively.

"No," said Quint.

"Why? You know how mad Pop'll get if he finds out you
wouldn't help? It's not good for him to get mad."

"I don't want her around," Quint answered stolidly. "My place is no place for a lady."

"This girl," Jerry offered slyly, "is no lady—or she wouldn't be in this mess."

"Living alone with me won't help her reputation," Quint countered, frowning darkly.

"She obviously doesn't give a hoot about her reputation," Jerry argued. "Besides, you're so far in the boondocks, who'll know she's there? If anybody meets her, say she's a cousin or something."

"Listen," Quint said with vehemence. "I don't want her and I won't take her."

Jerry looked craftily at his lean and stubborn older brother. "Know what?" he drawled. "I think you're scared. What's the matter—afraid you can't handle her? Afraid she'll get you?"

"Don't want her. Won't take her," Quint repeated doggedly, jamming his hands in the back pockets of his worn jeans.

"Your father's going to be so disappointed and upset!" moaned Mrs. Petitjean. "To think he barely escaped death, and now you won't help him. You don't care about people, Quinton—you just care about your old—your old—" She broke off in a hoot of teary despair.

"Yeah," Jerry sighed, looking at the sobbing Mrs. Petitjean. "That's what Pop's going to say. Only he won't bawl. He'll roar."

Quint swore again.

Five minutes later, jaw set like a steel trap, eyes dark with anger, he was driving toward the Little Rock airport. His van was battered and dirty, and he felt the same way.

He'd hardly slept the night before. When they'd called him about the accident the previous afternoon, he'd been splitting logs for a new deer paddock down on the Flirta-

tion River. He was filthy, his clothes stiff with day-old sweat
and his faded jeans torn at the knee. His blue plaid shirt had
two buttons missing from the front. His cowboy boots were
caked with dirt, and the Stetson jammed on his dark head
had seen better days. He hadn't shaved for two days. He
didn't look like a millionaire's son, he looked like a bum,
and an evil-tempered bum at that.

Maybe the girl would take one look and be scared back to
Washington.

He figured he wouldn't have any trouble picking her out
of the crowd getting off the plane. She'd be the one who'd
look like a floozy, only a very expensive floozy. Lord, he
hated a flirty woman. The only flirtation he liked was his
river, and it was a different kind of flirtation—untamed,
dangerous, full of secrets. A little bit, people had hinted
darkly, like himself.

MIRANDA SAT hunched in her seat, sad and frustrated as the
plane began its descent into Little Rock. Her father hadn't
troubled to come to the airport to see her off. Jaqueline also
refused to come because she said it would make her too sad.
Besides, she had an important meeting.

So it was Buford who saw her off and hugged her goodbye. She felt as if she were being sent to Siberia.

It wasn't fair, she thought wanly. She didn't know who
was sending the letters or why. She hadn't dated many boys
at college this year, and few more than twice.

She knew she had a reputation for being too fun-loving
and flighty, but she couldn't believe she had made anybody
angry enough to write the letters. Yet the letters had started
coming, almost daily, during the last month of school. They
kept coming when she went home to Washington. They were
all postmarked New York, which made them the more puzzling, especially when the writer always made a point of in-

sisting he was watching her. Buford explained that for a small fee, anybody, crazy or not, could have mail posted out of New York.

The whole business made her feel empty and scared and somehow soiled, but her father's only reaction was his angry accusation she had brought the disaster on herself.

Her mood worsened when the pudgy executive beside her tried to flirt with her. She had to be almost rude to him.

Why did it always have to be like this? she thought morosely. When she was younger, she'd enjoyed the attention her looks brought. She was admired, a sensation so novel it made her giddy. But her father and Jaqueline had warned her so often that people were interested only in her looks or her influence that she often wondered if it were true.

When the plane landed and the passengers rose, Miranda was infuriated to feel an intimate pat on her bottom. She whirled angrily and saw her plump neighbor directly behind her, smiling smugly. Resisting the desire to bang him over the head with her carry-on case, she sidestepped deftly out of his way, trying not to let the incident rankle. But it did, as it was the kind of encounter for which she'd be accused of flirting—and that just wasn't true.

When Miranda strode off the plane, she was in a mood so vile she thought she could probably stand up to Duke Wilcox with no trouble at all. A whole platoon of marines would not intimidate her.

She kept her chin up. Her cheeks were flushed, her eyes flashing. But as she approached the waiting area she stopped, suddenly hesitant.

She had expected to pick Duke Wilcox out of the waiting crowd immediately. He was such an enormous man, and time could not have changed his bulldog face that much. But she saw no one resembling him.

Then she noticed a man who loomed above the crowd. He was broad in the shoulders and lean everyplace else, and he looked like some sort of cowboy—a disreputable one at that. Although he had striking, deep blue eyes, they were cold and judgmental, even from this distance. He was unshaven and his clothes were dirty—even torn. He stared at her with what seemed pure dislike. Then he started walking toward her, never taking his eyes from her face.

Oh, no, thought Miranda. *Not him. Please. He looks like he should be walking down the main street of some Western town at high noon, ready to try his fast draw. Not him. Please.*

CHAPTER THREE

QUINT SPOTTED her immediately. She was tall, with wind-swept, honey-blond hair. She wore some kind of eye-popping turquoise pants outfit. The sleeves were like bat wings, and although the top was baggy, it didn't disguise that she was a girl of surpassing shapeliness. She had a wide choker necklace that glittered, and matching earrings flashed discreetly from the darker golden streaks of her hair. A crazy gold-colored bag hung from her shoulder and she held a white carry-on case that looked expensive enough to have dollar signs printed all over it.

A spoiled woman, he thought with distaste. And she'd marched into the place, her head held up proudly as if she owned Little Rock, as if she knew and enjoyed the stir her looks were bound to make. He remembered his original assessment. This creature wasn't in trouble. She was trouble, and looked like she loved it.

When her eyes met his, though, she looked at him first with curiosity, then disapproval, then dismay.

He ambled toward her lazily, enjoying the rising horror in her eyes. They were nice eyes, he admitted, a funny smoky gray green, with lashes to break a man's heart. But she needed taking down a peg or two, and since the job had fallen to him, he decided to do it right.

At last he stood next to her, looking down into her eyes; her face had gone pale beneath its tan. "Miss Mason?" he drawled.

She blinked, suspicious and disoriented. "Yes."

"Quint Wilcox. My father's had an accident. I'll be watching out for you till he's well. It may be a while."

Miranda looked him up and down in distrust. He had an acceptable face—rather handsome really, under the stubble—but was so slovenly dressed he should be ashamed to be seen in public. His black Stetson was dented and dusty, his shirt spattered with dry mud, and the knee was torn out of his jeans. But he looked as arrogant and in control as if he were wearing the uniform of a crown prince.

She dragged her eyes away from his mud-caked boots and back to his face. "I—hope your father isn't badly hurt," she managed to say, although it was hard to imagine anything capable of hurting Duke Wilcox.

"Leg broken. Accident with a truck," Quint said laconically. He reached over and took her carry-on case.

"Oh," Miranda said, feeling strangely numb all over. "Will—you be driving the truck now?"

He gave her a look that indicated he thought she was insane. He said nothing.

"Your father," she said, not liking his stare. "He's a truck driver, isn't he? I mean, did he wreck the truck or what? Or do you drive it now?"

Oh, Lord, Quint thought, she hadn't even bothered to find out anything about Duke or Deerfield Trucking before she came down. No wonder she was looking at him as if he were a scurvy peasant. He should have figured she was a snob on top of everything else.

"No," he replied with a sardonic twist of the truth. "You might say my brother drives the truck. You got more luggage?"

"Well, of course." Miranda looked at him with indignation. Jaqueline had practically insisted she pack half her wardrobe. "Well, what do you do, if you don't drive the truck? Are you a—a cowboy or something?"

"No," he said shortly. He started walking toward the baggage-claim area. She hurried after him. Her own legs were long, but she had trouble keeping up with him.

"Well, what do you do?" she asked. With his build it was obviously something physical.

He glanced down at her. It would be easier to show her than tell her. "I haven't figured out a name for what I do," he said. "Mostly I go my own way."

"Oh," she said sarcastically. "How informative. I assume you go your own way in Cherry Creek."

"Nope," he said, and kept walking.

"Well, where then?" she demanded. "Everybody thinks I'm going to Cherry Creek. Where are you taking me?"

"No place," he muttered, not bothering to look at her.

"What do you mean, 'no place'?" she insisted. She stopped, put her hands on her hips and glared at him. He ignored her and kept striding on.

She ran to catch up. "If I'm not going to Cherry Creek, where am I going?" she asked with some spirit, trying to keep pace with him. "And don't tell me 'no place' because that's a pretty rude answer, if you want my opinion."

He tossed her a glance that told her he didn't want her opinion. "It's no place because there's no town," he said. "There's nothing. Just woods. And the river. The Flirtation River. I've got a rural route number."

They had reached the luggage carousels, and for once the suitcases were spilling out in record time.

"I'm supposed to go into the woods with you? Alone?" she asked in true dismay.

"You're safe," he said without emotion. "Nobody can find you there. Which suitcase is yours?"

Miranda's shoulders sank. Cherry Creek had sounded bad enough, but at least it was a town. At least Duke Wilcox talked, even if he did so in a loud voice. Now she was going to be living in a forest, probably in a cave, with Mr. Strong and Silent. Well—one good thing. She was certain that she'd be safe—at least from him, because he acted as if he despised her without even knowing her.

She looked unhappily at the suitcases. "That one," she murmured dismally. "And that one. And that one and the garment bag. And the trunk."

He gave her a look that informed her he preferred women who traveled light, but he gathered up the baggage, grim resignation on his face. He managed to stack everything on one luggage cart and started wheeling it toward the parking lot. "Is this all?" he asked with the mocking lift of one dark brow. "Or is there more coming on the next cargo plane?"

She tossed her head and didn't bother to answer. She almost told him he could take a little more interest in clothes himself. He might not be a bad-looking man if he mastered the secrets of soap, water and clean laundry.

She plunged further into depression when she saw his van. It was, if possible, more disreputable than he was. He opened the back and flung her suitcases inside without ceremony. He did condescend to open the passenger door for her.

She sat down gingerly, pushing a dirty blanket out of her way. Strange contraptions littered the floor at her feet. He got in and slammed his door. She wrinkled her nose. The van smelled horrible.

"Good grief," she said in despair. "What is this? It smells like you had a bear in here or something." She tried to roll down her window, but it was stuck.

To her surprise, he gave a short laugh.

"What's so funny?" she demanded.

"I did," he said, putting the van in gear. It lurched off as roughly as she feared it would.

"Did what?" she asked impatiently.

"Have a bear in here," he replied.

"I don't believe you," she said imperiously. He was the most disagreeable man she'd ever met.

"Don't," he said. It was all he said for the rest of the trip.

They drove, it seemed, for hours. Outside Little Rock the evening fell quickly into an almost supernatural darkness. Mountains blocked the faint light of the stars. Miranda's mind worked furiously. She had to get out of this. Her father was angry with her, certainly, but he couldn't want her hidden on some horrid river with this—this cowboy.

The van left the highway and lurched down a series of back roads, each rougher than the last. Just when the road became so rutted that Miranda felt as if she were on a circus ride, the van jolted into a clearing and stopped.

A light from a tall pole shone down on a small log cabin. She swallowed hard. The cabin looked primitive. And very small.

She could see the shadowy forms of other buildings beside it, and a strange series of fences. A black-and-white dog gamboled around the van and greeted Quint with lavish affection when he stepped down. He gave the dog a quick scratch between the ears, then opened Miranda's door.

She stepped from the van, the back of her neck prickling with apprehension. Outside the circle of light, the night seemed darker than ever. She could hear the gurgle of the river but other noises, too—strange grunts and howls and cries.

Nervously she watched Quint unload. She understood his displeasure; where, in the small cabin, would all her things fit? And what, she wondered, was in the woods, making those frightful sounds?

Suddenly something bumped her from behind, hard. She turned and saw a huge animal standing there, practically on top of her. She screamed. She screamed again.

Quint set down a suitcase in disgust and came up beside her. "Calm down," he said contemptuously. "It's Bump. He bumps people."

"What is it?" she cried, clinging to Quint's arm in spite of herself.

"A yearling deer," he replied. "He's harmless. He just likes attention." He reached out and stroked the creature.

A deer, she thought in puzzlement, still unconsciously clinging to Quint. Deer were wild. What was this one doing, standing tamely and accepting human caresses?

Then, out of the corner of her eye, she saw something moving jerkily in the darkness. It was chained and made a loud whimpering noise. "What's that?" she cried.

"Bear cub," he said calmly. Reaching down, he pried her hand from his arm. "You'll hear more from him—and the rest—before the night's over."

"Rest? What *rest*?" she asked, eyes widening.

He nodded toward the pens. "More deer. Birds, raccoons, foxes. Come on. Let's get this stuff inside."

She snatched up two of the smaller suitcases and followed him, anxious to escape the darkness and the animal sounds. The inside of the cabin was cramped and chaotic. Bunk beds stood against one wall, and the only other room seemed to be a bathroom, though a bedroom area was separated from the main room with a curtain. In the crowded kitchen area, a large box took up a section of precious space. In the box lay a spotted fawn, blinking in bewilderment at the light. A white cast covered its front leg.

"You can have the bedroom," Quint said, pushing the curtain back. He set her suitcases on the floor. She stood in bewilderment, looking at the little room. The bed took most of the space. The black-and-white dog stood beside her, staring up at her with curiosity, wagging its tail.

Quint returned with more suitcases, left and came in with the trunk. There was barely room enough for her to make her way to the bed.

She turned to him, looked again at the little fawn in its box and then up into his eyes. "What kind of place is this?" she asked in bewilderment.

"My place," he said, returning her stare coolly.

"I know that," she said impatiently. "But all these animals?"

"It's a rehabilitation center for wildlife," he answered.

"Wildlife? Even bears?" she asked in disbelief.

"Yeah. And endangered species."

"You're a—veterinarian?" she asked dubiously.

He nodded curtly. "Wild animal practice. Wounded. Orphaned."

She moved to the fawn in the box and reached down to pet it. It cringed slightly, looking as lost and confused as she felt.

But Quint's hand clamped on her wrist and he drew her back. "Don't," he said. "She's not a pet. She's got to go back to the wild. She can't trust humans. Or she'll end up like Bump—dependent."

"Sorry," she said crisply, rubbing her wrist. He hadn't hurt her physically, but her feelings, tumultuous already, were injured.

He gave her a cold look. "Make yourself at home," he said gruffly. "I've got to feed this thing, then call my brother to see how my father is."

"I don't intend to stay here, you know," she said, struggling to find her old spirit of defiance. "My father didn't send me down here to stay out in the sticks with some strange man and no chaperon."

"Fine," Quint answered, his voice expressionless. "This wasn't my idea. Go. The faster the better. Only not tonight. I need some sleep."

"He won't stand for it," she said, wanting to show Quint she could be as hard as he could. "Having me alone with a man."

"You're safe," he said out of the side of his mouth. "Your type doesn't interest me. And don't pretend to worry about your reputation. If you cared about it, you wouldn't be in this fix. Just go to bed. You can call your father in the morning."

"I will," she said, and marched into the bedroom with as much dignity as she could. She jerked the curtain shut. She opened one of the smaller suitcases and drew out a nightgown. It was an expensive one and suitably demure, she hoped, for camping out with a grouchy savage.

She set the suitcase on the floor, switched off the light and climbed into bed. She lay down and hugged the pillow.

But she couldn't sleep. The man's words hurt. He was like everybody else, taking it for granted that she was so wild she'd brought retribution upon herself. She didn't know who was writing the stupid letters or why. She only knew they were ruining her life.

Here she was, in this wilderness, and if she knew her father, he would probably make her stay. He would say she was exactly where she belonged—in a place for wild things, guarded by a cold-eyed keeper.

QUINT FED the fawn. Then, bone weary, he called Jerry, who said Duke's condition was stable, and there was no reason for Quint to return to the hospital. Jerry jokingly asked him about how the mantrap was doing in captivity. Quint replied curtly that she was worse than he'd expected.

He hung up the phone, ready to sleep long and hard, even on the uncomfortable bunk. He'd wait until tomorrow to shower, so he washed as best he could at the bathroom sink.

He usually slept naked, but out of deference to the girl, he put on a pair of clean jeans and climbed onto the bed. He lay in the darkness. He was worried about his father, and he didn't like having his own solitude interrupted by his unwanted guest.

But he knew he had been harder on her than he had any right to be. He told Jerry she was worse than he expected, yet she hadn't been. It had just been the way she got off that plane, like she was royalty or something, that irked him.

Yet something about her troubled him, as if in her way she were as frightened and defenseless as that wounded fawn in the corner. No, he thought. Impossible. Not from what he knew about her.

He tried to dismiss her from his thoughts. But then he heard a muted noise. It was a tiny sound, but he had preternaturally sharp hearing. He could have sworn she was crying and trying to be quiet about it, hiding her head under the covers or something.

Damn! he thought, and punched the pillow. She probably was crying. He'd be glad when she called her father and got out of there.

Why had his father got mixed up in this? Especially since he didn't like the Senator . . . why bother with his daughter? Was it something Duke remembered about her as a child in Cambasia? Duke seemed tough, but he was a notorious softy where children were concerned. Could he have possibly been fond of her? Or, Quint thought with disquieting intuition, had Duke felt sorry for her? And if so, why? Perhaps, he thought uneasily, Duke liked the girl simply out of spite, because he disliked the Senator so much. But that wasn't like him. Duke was a forthright man.

In the darkness the fox kits yapped, and the great horned owl shrieked. Frogs sang along the riverbank, the crickets chirred wildly.

He had an image of Miranda lying in the darkness, listening to the sounds, cringing at each one. He wished he hadn't heard her crying. He needed to ignore her, he told himself.

But when he awoke at dawn, cramped from the narrow bunk, the first thing he remembered was that she was there, in his life, in his cabin, in his room, in his bed. He groaned.

Rising, he gave in to the temptation to take a glimpse of her. He pushed back the curtain to the bedroom slightly. Her hair spread in gold disarray upon the pillow. Her nightgown was white, high necked with billowing sleeves cuffed in lace. It gave her a startling air of youth and innocence. Her arms were crossed on her breast, as if even in sleep she were trying to protect herself from something.

He let the curtain fall back into place. He wished he hadn't taken that forbidden glimpse of her, defenseless in her sleep. For the first time he realized precisely how beautiful she was.

CHAPTER FOUR

MIRANDA AWOKE at midmorning to the snarl of a chain saw outside. Disoriented, she felt a familiar sense of panic: *where am I this time?* The Senator had moved his family and changed Miranda's schools so often that she sometimes had attacks of anxiety when she awoke in a strange place.

Where am I? She sat up, heart pounding. Then she remembered. She was cast into the wilderness. The chain saw was probably manned by that unshaven cowboy who was caustic when he bothered to talk at all.

She was going to get up, shower, wash her hair, then call her father and plead with him to send her anywhere—even a convent.

In the bathroom she was bewildered to find neither shower nor bathtub. It figured, she thought bleakly. Tarzan probably bathed under a waterfall if he bothered to bathe at all. She scrubbed herself by the sink and brushed her hair until its gleam convinced her she could probably go one more day without a shampoo. She saw no point of putting on makeup for a grump, a bear, a dog and a deer, so simply dabbed lip gloss on her full mouth and called it quits.

She went to her room and explored her suitcases. The Senator disapproved of jeans, so she owned only one pair, which she decided to wear. They were expensive, the back pockets decorated with a design of rhinestone hearts. She slipped on a white crocheted sweater. Then she chose white sandals and decided she was ready to rough it—at least until she could make her escape.

When she came out of the bedroom, Quint was standing in the kitchen. He held a coffee cup in one hand, and with the other he wiped a faded bandanna across the back of his neck. His eyes narrowed slightly when he saw her, but his face remained wooden.

Miranda felt her own gray-green eyes widen in surprise. He had shaved and showered—where? she wondered. His jeans were clean, and so was his pale blue shirt. He had on different boots, polished. He was, she saw, a handsome man in a lean and startling way.

"Good morning," she said, eyeing him warily. For some reason her heart had started beating fast again.

He took a sip of coffee, keeping his gaze trained on her. She looked as if she were dressed for a day of lazing on a sailboat or something, he thought. But that luxuriant blond hair shone like sunlight on wheat, and she had the kind of face that could shake a man down to his heel bones.

So he wasn't talking, was he? Miranda thought irritably. She refused to be intimidated. "Is there more coffee?" she asked.

He nodded brusquely, indicating a battered pot on the stove. She walked past him, paused a moment to look down at the fawn, who was sleeping fitfully. He frowned at her. She tossed her head. "Don't worry," she said, reaching into the cupboard to search for a cup. "I'm not going to touch your precious deer. I won't corrupt her. I just want some coffee and then I'm going to call my father and tell him I cannot, under any circumstances, stay here."

She finally discovered a clean mug, though it had a broken handle. She poured herself a cup of brew as black as tar. She cleared a pile of zoological journals off a kitchen chair and sat down at the table.

He watched her with that same impassive face. She drank from the cup, grimaced slightly, then looked up at him.

"Stop staring," she demanded.

He didn't stop. His dark blue eyes practically bored through her. He sat down across from her. "We're stuck with each other," he said with cold disgust.

"What do you mean?" she asked, raising her chin and giving him a suspicious look. "I'm going to call my father and—"

"Your father and I already talked," he snapped. "Or rather, I listened while he ranted. Everybody's talked to everybody. My brother and your father. My father and yours. And somebody named Buford called—"

"Buford?" Miranda asked. She didn't like the displeasure in Quint's strongly boned face, and she didn't understand what he was saying.

"I've talked to my father—or rather listened while he yelled. Then I called my brother so I could yell at somebody. We're stuck. You're staying here."

"What?" she said in disbelief. "No! I can't. My father would never let me."

"My brother, Jerry, called your father last night. He took the liberty of saying I was a cross between Sir Galahad the chaste, Saint Gerald the pure and a hermit monk. Made me sound like a wimp or a weirdo or both," he muttered, then swore.

"My father certainly wouldn't accept—" Miranda began, but he only frowned more antagonistically.

"So your father called my father, who was full of pain-killers. Pop assured him that I'm harmless—why everybody suddenly thinks I'm harmless, I don't know. Pop swore that if I laid so much as a finger on you, he would personally bring your father my head on a platter."

"But—" Miranda tried to protest.

He cut her off, his eyes growing more offended by the second. "Then this Buford called. I told him you were safe with me. He said the question might be whether I was safe with you."

"Buford said that?" Miranda asked, outraged. She had always considered Buford her friend. Why was he suddenly misinforming the world that she was a dangerous siren? All she had ever done was a little harmless flirting. She vowed then and there she would die before she flirted with Quint Wilcox. She would never give him the satisfaction.

"So everybody's called," snarled Quint, "and I told them I wouldn't touch you with a ten-foot pole. This seemed to delight everyone, especially your father. I do not, incidentally, like your father."

Stung, Miranda shrugged self-consciously. "Daddy isn't at his best when he's talking about me."

"He sounds like a cold-blooded bastard. He couldn't have been more delighted when I told him you hated it here," Quint said, anger flashing deep in his eyes. "Excuse me, but I find it strange that you don't want to be here, I don't want you here, and he couldn't be happier."

"What else did Buford say?" she asked bitterly. "That you should chain me to the sink and feed me on bread and water?"

He shifted in his chair uncomfortably, staring into the murk of his coffee. "He said you weren't such a bad kid if somebody would teach you responsibility. He said to watch out for you."

"Watch out for me? What did he mean? That you should beware of me—or take care of me?"

"Both," Quint said darkly.

He sat in infuriated silence and Miranda thought gloomily of what Buford, with all of his psychological quackery, would tell Quint. Buford would make her sound like an immature and neurotic twit who could do nothing more complicated than bat her eyelashes. The thought of Buford talking about her that way made her want to cry again. But Miranda had learned long ago to cry only when she was alone. It was too humiliating to let people see how much, and how often, she could be hurt.

"How did I miss all this?" she said, trying to sound cool yet defiant. "The phone must have rung all morning."

"You sleep like a sloth." Quint shrugged irritably.

She didn't find the image flattering. "I'm going to call my father anyway," she retorted. "He hasn't heard my side of this, and I—"

He looked up at her sharply. "No," he said, his cobalt eyes intent.

"No what?" she asked in confusion. She pushed her coffee cup away. Her stomach hurt, as it often did lately.

"He doesn't want you to call," Quint said, too quietly. "He doesn't want to talk to you about this. He'll write—when he has some time."

She felt as if she had been slapped. Biting the inside of her lip, she struggled to maintain her self-control. Her back was straight with her determination to appear unfazed.

"So," she said, her voice flippant. She reached for her coffee cup and clinked it against Quint's. "We're stuck. Sorry. Nobody seems to want me around. Don't worry. I'll pull my own weight around here."

His face had become the same dispassionate mask again. "What's that mean?" he asked dubiously.

"I mean I'll work. I'll help you. I can't just sit around all day."

"You?" he scoffed. "Work?"

"Well," she said, wounded but refusing to show it, "I have on my work clothes, don't I?"

He looked at her, sitting there in her crocheted top, her earrings, her flimsy sandals and her hundred-dollar jeans.

"Work clothes?" He actually laughed.

"What's so funny?" she demanded.

"Lady," he said, "you got diamonds all over the seat of your britches."

"So what?" she said, giving him a superior stare. She was suddenly determined to make him respect her even if the effort killed her.

He said nothing. He only stood, gave her a wry, one-sided smile and started heating the fawn's formula. "Fine," he muttered at last. "If you want to work, go out in your diamond pants and feed the foxes."

"Fine yourself," she said. "Pray tell me what one feeds a fox."

"Dead chicks," he answered. "They're thawing on the counter. Go ahead. Unless you don't want to touch a dead chick."

Miranda didn't, but she wouldn't give him the satisfaction of showing it. "I will view them simply as raw foodstuff," she said airily. She rose confidently but wrinkled her nose with distaste as she picked up the dish towel with the fuzzy yellow birds on it. She swung out the back door as if she knew exactly what she was doing.

"Don't pet those fox kits and don't talk to them," he called after her. "They aren't puppies. They have to go back to the wild."

She heard him but didn't bother to answer.

He watched the light flashing off the rhinestone hearts on the seat of her jeans and shook his head again. He looked down at the fawn. "That girl," he said, "has got a lot to learn."

The fawn looked up with its eyes of total innocence.

But Quint, whose eyes had lost their innocence long ago, took another look out the screen door, watching those hearts walk away from him.

QUINT WAS RIGHT. Miranda had a lot to learn, and by noon she had learned a good deal. She found, for instance, that foxes are more shy than sly, and a young red fox is gray. She learned to stay clear of all the deer except the too-tame Bump. Even a wounded deer can kick with enough force to seriously injure.

She learned that as cute as a bear cub was, it had formidable claws and teeth. She learned semitame raccoons loved to pull human hair and twist human ears to see if they were removable. They also liked to thrust their little fingers into her crocheted sweater trying to extract the threads. If she tried to ignore Bump, he butted her to gain her attention. She discovered that an eagle, even wing shot and caged, was one of nature's most awesome sights.

The worst thing she learned was about crows. Quint had a crow named Ratso. Ratso had been orphaned, raised by Quint and released, but refused to leave. He stayed around the cabin, making as much trouble as he could. He liked to dive-bomb the bear and tease the raccoons, but even Ratso had enough sense to leave the eagle alone.

Miranda could not tell if Ratso loved or hated her. He liked to fly down, sit on her shoulder and play with her earring, trying to pull it off. The first time he did it, she screamed. By the fourth time, she shook her fist at him, drove him off and called him a robbing idiot.

"Robbing idiot! Robbing idiot!" shrieked Ratso in delight, flying to the safety of a cedar tree to plan his next attack. Like all crows he was clever, and like many, he was an excellent mimic.

Worst, Ratso adored the rhinestones on the seat of Miranda's jeans. One of the jobs Quint assigned her was the evil-smelling one of scrubbing out the empty fox shelters. She had to do this on her hands and knees, and Ratso delighted in making air raids on her derriere, trying to steal the rhinestones. Every time he pecked at one, she had to restrain herself from crying out in surprise and outrage.

Quint, shirtless now in the spring heat, was finishing the new deer paddock. He smiled cryptically when Ratso swooped down to try to pillage Miranda's bejeweled hindquarters.

When they broke for lunch, Miranda stood grumpily at the cluttered kitchen counter. "Give me a sharp knife," she demanded.

Quint, still shirtless, his bronzed torso gleaming with perspiration, looked at her. "That bad?" he asked mildly. "Going to end it all?"

"No," she snapped. "I'm going to cut these stupid pockets off." She had already taken off her earrings. He handed her a paring knife, and she began to hack ineffectually at her sparkling back pockets.

He watched her with self-satisfied amusement. "You're going to cut out the whole seat of your pants," he said with a smug grin. "Here. Let me." He took the knife from her, and she had little choice but to lean against the counter. Deftly he slashed off the offending pockets, but his sure hands moving across her hips gave Miranda a very peculiar sensation.

"There," he said, laying the pockets on the counter. "And I see you took the earrings off. Good. Crows love shiny things." He pushed back the thick gold of her hair but held its softness a moment too long, and her heart made the same kind of joyous bound that Bump took from time to time.

"Your ear is bleeding," he said, his voice suddenly quiet. "Ratso really hurt you."

Still he hadn't moved his hand. "It didn't hurt that much," Miranda said. With Quint shirtless and that close, his hand in her hair, her voice seemed to choke in her throat. "I'm not a sissy," she said, her throat still constricted.

He pushed her hair a little farther back, gently, so it didn't touch the slight tear in her earlobe. "Sit down," he ordered. "I'll get some antiseptic."

She was right, he thought ironically, going to the bathroom for the first-aid kit. She might have a lot of flaws, but cowardice wasn't among them. For a city girl, she'd taken the animals in surprisingly competent stride, even Ratso. On more than one occasion, Ratso's surprise attacks had sent strong men running for shelter, yelling for shotguns and SWAT teams.

She also worked hard, which surprised him. He'd had her feed the fox kits and clean the empty cages to test her. He thought she'd throw a tantrum or balk, but she went at everything with impressive energy. She had phenomenal energy. Maybe that was part of her problem.

When he returned with the antiseptic, she was sitting at the table, watching the fawn but not touching it. She had a pensive look on her face. He suddenly felt a twinge of sympathy for her. Her father had sounded like a cold-blooded bastard.

But when she looked up at him with those unfathomable gray-green eyes, he tried to banish such charitable thoughts. He dressed her torn earlobe roughly. He tried to ignore the softness of her skin and the silky feel of her hair. Such things could lead to nothing but trouble. He was out here on the river because he'd had enough trouble in his life.

She winced at his hardhanded ministrations but said nothing. Brusquely he pushed her shining hair back into place. "You'll live," he said uncaringly, then set about putting lunch together for them.

The affair was not elegant. They ate in tense silence. Sometimes Miranda caught him watching her as intently as if she were some new and rather dangerous animal who had fallen under his care. That look and his silence made her skin prickle.

"You could be a little more communicative," she accused at last. "You could have warned me about that rotten crow. Or told me just how bad a fox smells. Or how hard Bump can bump."

He ignored her gibe. "Pass the mayonnaise."

She pushed the jar toward him across the faded tablecloth. "Just what are you doing out here anyway?" she demanded, staring at him through her blond-streaked bangs. "I mean, obviously this is some kind of halfway house for wild animals in trouble, but what's the point? Are you a forest ranger, too? Whose property is this? The government's? And why don't you clean this place up? It's a mess." She regarded the clutter with distaste.

"I live the way I like to. My father owns the land. Someday I'll build a real house. And the point is, Pop's interested in trucking and so's my brother. But Pop's also interested in the environment, and so am I. This is Pop's favorite project—wildlife protection. It's also a tax write-off. Jerry will manage the truckline. I build and manage the wildlife center."

"Tax write-off?" she said suspiciously. "I thought your father was a truck driver."

"He owns the line," Quint said curtly. "His father started it. Pop left the marines and took over when the old man died."

The news didn't seem to impress her as much as it did most women. He supposed she was used to families far more rich and powerful than the Wilcoxes.

"Where do they all come from—the animals, I mean?" she asked. She had always liked animals but never owned one. Jaqueline was allergic to anything with fur or feathers.

"From everywhere," Quint said, cynicism creeping in his voice. "This little gal—" he nodded at the fawn in the box "—got caught in a trap. We've got a poacher around here. He shot the eagle, too, I'm pretty sure. He's responsible for a lot of wounded animals. Authorities can't catch the bastard. Neither can I. His name's Slayton. If I ever do get him red-handed, I'll shake his goddamned teeth out before I turn him over to the law."

Miranda regarded him warily. There was real bitterness in his voice, and she knew he meant what he said.

His voice became more casual, almost bored. "The rest come from all over. Some get hit by cars. Some orphaned. Some poisoned. Some were adopted, then abandoned. If I can get them into shape to fend for themselves, I put them back in the wild. If they're too hurt to go back but can live, I give them shelter."

"What about Bump?" Miranda asked. Bump's demands for affection were exasperating, but he was a beautiful animal and fascinated Miranda.

"Bump," Quint said with a disgusted sigh, "is the worst kind of case. Somebody found him when he was a fawn, spoiled him, then got tired of him. They dumped him on me, but Bump can't go back to the wild. He's dependent on humans. He trusts them. Eventually he's going to walk up to somebody in hunting season and get his head blown off."

"No!" Miranda protested in horror.

He nodded without emotion. "Happens all the time to animals like Bump. So it's important the wildlings—that's what they're called—don't get attached to humans. For their own safety, they have to fear us."

Her face got that distant, sad look he noticed sometimes. He sensed, in spite of her reputation, she was one of those women with a strong nurturing sense. She kept looking longingly at the fawn.

"If you've got to pet something," he said gruffly, getting up from the table, "confine yourself to the dog—Boots. But not too much. He's a working dog—a Border collie."

She sat silent, as if looking deep inside herself and seeing only emptiness. He cleared away his plate and the remaining food. "And there's Bump," he said, sounding harsher than he felt. "Pet him as much as you want. He thrives on it. Who knows, maybe something else will turn up that you can love."

Her eyes rose slowly to meet his. *Maybe it will,* she thought. For the first time in her life she realized why all the boys and men she knew had bored her. They were shallow, silly, soft. The man standing before her was none of these. Nor was he, like her father and his friends, interested in power for the sake of power or money for the sake of money. This was a man different from any she had ever known.

He swallowed, as if suddenly nervous. "Why don't you stay inside awhile?" he said gruffly. "You're not used to this heat. Or work. You'll wear yourself out."

She cleared her section of the table. "I spent six years in Cambasia," she said stubbornly. "And two in India. I can stand heat. I might as well help with the grunt work. I'm not good for much else."

He shrugged coldly and let her follow him back outside. But his thoughts were troubled. Damn, he thought. On the surface she could act like the Queen of Sheba, but deep down she didn't seem to think much of herself. What on earth had the cretin of a senator done to her? And why?

By three in the afternoon Miranda realized the crocheted top didn't qualify as work clothing and it was too hot to work in her jeans. She went inside, and gritting her teeth, she cut the legs off her jeans to make them into cutoffs and changed into a short-sleeved cotton blouse.

She pinned her hair up in a topknot and wished she had a pair of work gloves. She'd been throwing hay to the deer, and her hands were getting sore from the rough wood of the pitchfork handle.

She went back outside. Quint had almost finished the new deer paddock. The sweat gleamed on his coppery body as he hammered wire to the posts. He had abandoned his Stetson and knotted a blue bandanna around his forehead. He looked as natural and strong as one of the tall pines that protected the cabin.

She filled a battered washtub at the outside faucet and prepared for her next job. Quint had given her a bottle of terrible-smelling medicine and told her he had to give an adult fox its mange bath. Miranda, who had never bathed anything but herself, was still trying to figure out how he would do it without getting both hands chewed off.

She pulled the heavy tub into the sunlight so the water would warm, then started measuring out the odoriferous medicine.

Quint was hammering the last of the fencing into place when a pickup truck pulled into the clearing. Miranda, feeling like one of Macbeth's ragged witches stirring an evil brew, looked up.

The truck, with an official emblem on its side, pulled to a stop and a man in a tan uniform got out. He looked about forty, was stockily built and had a round, pleasant face.

He studied Miranda with polite puzzlement and then frank pleasure. "Harry McIver," Quint said, introducing him to Miranda. "Wildlife management supervisor. Harry's sons took over here as soon as Pop was hurt." He turned to the man. "Haven't even had time to send thanks," he said.

"Boys don't mind," Harry said, not taking his eyes from Miranda. "Pleased to meet you, Miss—?"

Quint looked at Miranda. "This is my—uh—cousin. Miranda Wilcox. She's—uh—going to be helping me awhile."

Harry McIver removed his hat and beamed at her. "Pleased to meet you, ma'am," he said. "Never knew there were any good looks in the Wilcox family—reckon you got them all."

Harry, who quickly managed to inform Miranda he was a widower, couldn't seem to stop grinning at her. It made her uncomfortable. He pointedly mentioned again that he was a widower and had been for some time. She knew with a sinking heart she'd made another unwanted conquest.

She was equally nonplussed by Quint's awkward explanation of her as his cousin. Like most honest men he was a poor liar, and she was surprised Harry McIver believed the ridiculous story.

Harry finally forced himself to pull his attention away from Miranda. He gave Quint a rueful look. "It's startin'," he said. "You don't think this truck is empty, do you?"

Quint shook his head. He had seen the cages and boxes in the truck bed and knew better.

"First," Harry said with chagrin, "some little girl asked me to bring you these. Wind blew a tree down." He thrust a cardboard box at Quint.

Quint looked inside and swore. "Squirrels," he said without enthusiasm. He handed the box to Miranda. "What else we got, Harry?"

Miranda stared down at the tiny velvety bodies in the cotton-lined box. The squirrels were hardly larger than house mice, their eyes still closed.

Harry was on the back of the truck. He handed down a large cage draped with an old blanket. "Another orphan fawn," he said. "Tranquilized. I think a poacher got its mother. Slayton, I bet. I'd love to catch that bastard."

"Damn," Quint said, his powerful muscles straining as he set the cage on the ground. "At least we needed another fawn. They're easier to free if you've got two."

"This one'll be even more fun," Harry said, handing down a box with breathing holes drilled in it. "Bobcat. Looks like it got hit—dislocated hip maybe."

Quint swore again. "I hate to see a hurt cat. We can't afford to lose any."

"You're telling me," Harry sighed. "And the pièce de résistance," he continued. "Wait till you see this. Got his mouth tied shut and tranquilized him good. Didn't want this old boy wakin' up en route. Careful. He's heavy."

"We can handle him," Quint said. He leaped up beside Harry in the truck, and once again his muscles rippled and strained as the two men struggled with an enormous gray object swathed in ropes. As they lowered it from the back of the truck, Miranda's stomach lurched in alarm. The beast, its dragonlike eyes glazed and open, was an alligator, almost five feet long.

"What happened to him?" she asked Harry in awe.

"Front foot's gone," Harry said, glad to have her attention. "Might have been a trap or a shot—Slayton again, probably."

"I didn't know there were alligators around here," Miranda said with a shudder. She cast a nervous glance toward the river.

"They introduced some up north," Harry said with a smile. "To control the beaver population. But poachers like Slayton killed most of them. This old boy's a rarity. I wouldn't be scared, ma'am."

Miranda shivered in spite of Harry's assurance. She watched the two men strain to carry the huge reptile into a barred enclosure with a shallow pond in its corner. Mischievous deer and feisty crows were one thing, a full-grown alligator was another. She stepped up to the edge of the pen to watch Quint remove some of the animal's bonds.

Quint bent over the big beast, examining it. He paid special attention to the injured leg, which looked infected.

He stood again. He looked at Harry solemnly, and the smaller man returned his concerned gaze. "This is real trouble," Quint said at last.

"Yeah," Harry said with resignation. "Can't let it loose with a missing foot. It'll never survive. No zoo's gonna want it. What will you do with it?"

"See if I can get a permit to give it to one of the universities," Quint sighed. "Some biology department with a good reptile collection. Which means a damned mountain of red tape." Both men shook their heads.

Harry finally said his goodbyes and made a point of inviting both Quint and "Cousin Miranda" over for supper some evening. Every time he looked at Miranda, he got that same dazed smile on his face.

As McIver's truck pulled away, Quint rubbed his bare shoulder. Wrestling the weight of the big gator must have challenged even his superior strength.

He looked down at Miranda and cocked a dark brow sardonically. "You got to Harry fast," he said dispassionately, "even if you do smell like fox dip."

"Well, I wasn't trying to," she said with honest protest. Surely Quint had seen she hadn't flirted with Harry in the slightest.

"I know," he said, looking away. "That's what's scary. Let me put the fawn in the house."

"Two fawns in the house?" Miranda asked.

"They feel safer there. Older ones need space, but the young ones want cover. Anyway, then I'll examine the bobcat and treat the gator, and afterward you can help me dip the fox."

"And what about these squirrels?" she asked, looking down at the gray mites curled in their box.

His smile disappeared. "You wanted something to fuss over. Nothing takes more fuss than a squirrel. Congratulations—Mom."

"Mom?" Miranda wailed, looking at the helpless things.

"Mom. A baby squirrel needs to be fed every two hours. Day and night."

"Joy," Miranda said gloomily. "And do you mind telling me how you give a fox a bath without it biting you to pieces?"

"Easy," he said. "I hypnotize it."

"Sure," she replied sarcastically, putting one hand on her hip and looking up at him. But for some eerie reason, she suddenly felt certain that he could hypnotize a fox, or anything else he wanted.

He glanced down, his face stony as usual. "Bring the squirrels in They're not safe in the open."

He carried the fawn into the kitchen. She followed him, holding the box carefully.

He watched her as she set the box on the desk and gently stroked the small animals' silky fur. The girl was harder to ignore than he thought possible. If she could reduce staid, sensible Harry McIver to a grinning idiot without doing a thing, how could she help driving a bunch of harebrained college boys wild? Maybe he'd misjudged her. He knew what it was to be judged harshly, and he'd sworn never to do it to anyone else. Just the thought that he was treating someone unfairly made him grim and uneasy.

Miranda glanced up and met his eyes in puzzlement. He looked inordinately stern. What a strange man, she thought—strong, gentle, but cold. She wondered if he had any real human warmth, and if he did, would he ever be interested in someone like her? No, she thought. He'd probably prefer her sister's type. She wished she was like Jaqueline—ladylike, sweet and totally good. But she wasn't. She was only troublesome, wild, gossiped-about Miranda.

As they went back out the door, his bare arm accidentally brushed hers. Both pulled back from the chance contact as from a small, potent electrical shock. Neither looked at the other. But Miranda's arm burned where his hard flesh had touched her.

Quint rubbed his arm as it tingled unnaturally. No, he told himself sternly. He didn't want to think about her that way. He didn't want to think about her at all.

But all afternoon, as she worked beside him, almost keeping pace with him, he found himself furtively watching her.

At day's end, he showed her the shallow, mossy cave with a warm spring pouring out through the rocks like a small waterfall. He told her brusquely that it was his shower, and she was delighted. He had wired lights within, and they twinkled on the stalactites and quartz formations. It was, Miranda thought, like having a shower in fairyland.

When she headed toward the cave with her towels and shampoo and scented soap, Quint mentally kicked himself because he couldn't help thinking of her golden body under the fall of that sparkling water. He stalked half a mile downstream, stripped and took a long swim in the river, whose May waters, unlike those of the cave, still had a slight chill.

Ratso the crow had followed him and sat on an oak branch overhanging the river. He cast his bright, mocking eye down at Quint, who kept submerging himself in the glacial water, then surfacing, gasping with cold.

"Ha!" chortled Ratso, as if he knew some infinitely amusing private joke. "Can't cool off! Can't cool off! Ha, ha, ha!"

Quint cast the crow a killing look. "Shut up," he growled, his teeth on edge.

Ratso jeered.

CHAPTER FIVE

MIRANDA EMERGED from the limestone cave feeling clean and vibrant. Quint had told her that the temperature of both the spring and the cave stayed constant year-round. They were cool in summer, warm in winter. Nature's own climate control, Miranda thought in admiration.

She walked the path back to the cabin. Her damp hair was bound in a towel, turbanlike, and her silky, peach-colored outfit was soft against her tingling skin. She felt alive all over, as if somebody had filled her bloodstream with stars.

Bump was waiting for her, standing in the center of the path. He tried to butt her playfully but quit when she stroked his velvety neck. He gazed at Miranda with his large, liquid eyes, and she couldn't help smiling. Keeping her arm around his neck, she walked back to the cabin. He stayed beside her as faithfully as a dog.

At the cabin she dried her hair and began feeding the baby squirrels with a doll bottle. They were, she saw, going to be a full-time job.

Quint came in, cast her a brief, unfriendly look and said nothing at all. He wore clean jeans and a fresh shirt, and his damp hair kept falling into his eyes. With a maximum of banging and clanging, he started making supper—if canned chili, canned tamales, canned chicken soup and stale corn chips could qualify as supper.

"Why don't you let me cook?" Miranda asked, slightly alarmed as he crashed about. He was already burning the chili.

"This is my place. I cook," he said shortly.

"You're scorching the soup," she told him. He'd just finished keeping the chili from overflowing like erupting lava.

He turned the flame off beneath the soup and tossed her a scowl. "I don't believe," he said sarcastically, "that you know how to cook. You probably never did anything more complicated than smear caviar on a cracker."

"I don't know how to cook," she replied, determined to give him as good as she got. "But I could do better than that with one hand behind my back."

He ignored her. He slammed plates and bowls on the table, then ladled out the chili and soup, which were scorched, and the tamales, which were still cold.

"Ugh," said Miranda, sitting down reluctantly.

"Eat," he commanded. He leveled his dark blue glare at her for a moment, then began to spoon up his chili.

She shuddered delicately and began eating. She didn't understand why his mood was so foul. Her earlier euphoria disappeared. For some reason, the two of them seemed to be back where they had started: in barely cloaked enmity.

At the end of the meal he pushed back his chair from the table and studied her critically. He dwelt a few seconds too long on the curves of her peach-colored tunic.

"That all you've got to wear?" he asked, nodding toward her clothing. "Stuff like that?"

"What if it is?" she returned defensively. She had no idea why he was so unfriendly and abrupt again.

He rose and started clearing the table. "Because you're going to ruin everything you own. This isn't the country club."

"It isn't?" she asked in mock surprise. "Mercy, I was fooled. Especially after the cuisine."

He wasn't amused. "I go to Little Rock Saturday to see my father. I'll take you shopping."

"You don't have to take me shopping," Miranda objected. She, too, had risen and was clearing her own place. "I can shop by myself, thank you."

"I'm supposed to keep my eye on you," he replied, obdurate.

Miranda sighed in exasperation. "Fine. Keep your eye on me. But do it while I'm washing these dishes. Please get out of the way. You made supper—such as it was."

She tried to forge past him, so she could wipe the kitchen counters. He wouldn't move. They suddenly seemed too close, the crowded kitchen too small. Miranda found herself breathing too quickly.

He stared down at her, his own breath slightly labored. With a tautly controlled slowness, he placed his hands firmly on her shoulders, close to her neck. She felt the warmth of his touch tantalizingly near her throat. He could not have affected her more if he had draped a lightning bolt on her shoulders.

She held her breath. His face grew even harder. He licked his lips, glanced briefly at hers. His grip tightened. Then, effortlessly, he turned her so she faced away from him. "Out," he said stonily. "Go." He released her, but she could still sense his nearness.

Miranda felt so giddy that her stomach began doing strange things. In fact, it hurt. She stepped away quickly, as if to protect herself. She bit her lip. For some odd reason, the way Quint had ejected her made tears spring to her eyes. She stopped by the window, hoping to see Bump. He was there, grazing by the riverbank in the twilight. Unconsciously she put her hand on her stomach.

Quint hadn't moved. He stood watching her. He clenched his hands into fists, then unclenched them, flexing his fingers. She looked unlike herself, standing there, too quiet, too full of uncertainty and doubt. He could have sworn he saw the glint of tears in her eyes. And she didn't look well; she appeared almost ill.

"Are you—okay?" he asked finally. His voice was low.

"I'm fine," she said, not letting herself look at him. "I'd just like to help, that's all."

She kept her slender hand clamped on her midsection.

"Are you sick or something?" he prodded.

She stared at Bump's graceful shape as if the deer were the most important thing in the world. "Oh," she said softly. "It's nothing. I just feel funny sometimes." She laughed self-consciously. "I get the tummy-bumbles. That's what Buford called it when we were little."

"It happens a lot?"

She shrugged again. "I usually don't pay attention. I've got other things on my mind."

"Like what?"

She stared out at Bump again. "Like those letters. And my father. And moving around all the time. And my sister."

There was an awkward beat of silence between them. "I never knew you had a sister," he said. "Did you steal all her thunder? Or is she just like you, and next week I'll have two of you on my hands?"

She tried to smile but could not. She kept looking out the window. "We're not at all alike. She never does anything wrong. She's very sensible. Dependable. Serious."

Her voice quavered slightly. She was glad twilight was falling fast and that the only light came from the kitchen. She felt strange, as if years of protective covering had been stripped from her, and she stood, uncovered and totally vulnerable.

She thought of Jaqueline and she thought of herself. Opposites, like night and day. She knew what she herself was—troublesome, volatile, too quick to act, to laugh, to do something flippant—and worst of all, she was useless.

She listened, half-numb, as Quint made overenergetic splashing sounds in the kitchen. She could almost see the twilight growing thicker.

"If you're just going to stand there," he grumbled at last, "you might as well dry the dishes. Or something."

A peace offering, she thought, surprised. For some reason he was making a peace offering, no matter how temporary. She pressed her lips together, trying to calm her turbulent emotions. "Sure," she said.

She returned to the kitchen and picked up an ancient dish towel. She felt odd standing next to him, as if he gave off some sort of pure, alarming, masculine radiation. But, just as strangely, as they stood together in the kitchen's small circle of light, she also felt something she had never before experienced. Even though Quint made a point of saying nothing to her, she felt as if she finally knew where she was, where she belonged, and that for the first time in her life she was totally safe—taken care of.

FRIDAY CAME. Miranda thought the days she had spent on the Flirtation River were the strangest of her life. They had passed with magical swiftness. She had quickly grown to love the Edenlike solitude of the river and caring for the animals.

She especially adored the troublesome Bump, who required her incessant affection. She loved the squirrel babies just as passionately, even though they were almost as demanding as human babies. During the night she had to awaken every two hours and feed them. She named them Desiree and Monique. When Quint heard that, he looked more disgusted than usual.

"They're pretty names," Miranda protested. "Little girls deserve pretty names."

He only shook his head and went out to chop wood. He chopped it furiously, as if it would help him forget something he desperately needed to forget.

Miranda continued to learn. Quint taught her how to "hypnotize" the foxes. Distract the fox, he told her, by waving one hand before its face, then grab it quickly by the scruff of the neck. A fox will lose its will to fight that way. She found out that bears are moody, raccoons tend to overeat, bobcats are vulnerable to colds, and an alligator, indestructible as it may seem, is dangerously prone to hepatitis.

She temporarily solved her wardrobe problem by wearing her short-skirted tennis dresses. Quint talked to her less than ever and seemed equally determined not to look at her. But sometimes, without warning, her eyes would meet his, and his gaze was so intent she felt jolted clear through.

When there was no work to be done with the animals, she cleaned up the cabin. "Don't," Quint said shortly, the first time he found her cleaning and tidying.

"This mess gets on my nerves," Miranda countered stubbornly. "I have to do something."

"Women," he muttered.

She ignored his gibe and wiped the cobwebs from the frame of the kitchen window. But when she turned to get a clean paper towel, he was standing there, watching her—his eyes so haunting and so piercing at the same time, almost as if the look carried with it some mysterious part of him. She thought about the way he'd watched her for the rest of the day. That night in bed she was filled with troubled restlessness. The spring night sang around her, as if to taunt her.

SATURDAY MORNING, Miranda fluttered with excitement. Quint was taking her back into the real world: Little Rock, with its skyscrapers, teeming traffic and bustling crowds.

Harry McIver's elder boy was coming to take care of the animals—except for the squirrels. Miranda refused to entrust Desiree and Monique to anyone else. She carried them in a small cage, where they curled sleeping in a nest of toweling. The cage along with a jar of formula and the squirrel's bottle all fit nicely in her oversized gold shoulder bag.

Quint, she noted with pleasure, was almost dressed up. A pair of khaki-colored chinos encased his long legs. His white oxford-cloth shirt dramatized the deepness of his tan. He had even traded his cowboy boots for an expensive pair of suede walking moccasins. But crisp and civilized as he looked, something in his lean face and deep-set eyes seemed slightly at odds with the rest of his clean-cut image, something a bit too independent, even a touch wild.

Most surprising of all, he had cleaned out the van, washed it and even polished it. Miranda looked at him in surprise, one eyebrow raised questioningly.

He shrugged as if it meant nothing and opened her door. Miranda, in her filmy white shirtwaist dress, gold choker and sandals, got in. Because she was returning to civilization she was dressed to the teeth, her golden hair swept high in a style that was both elegant and artfully unstudied.

Quint got in and cast her a brief, measuring look as she fastened her seatbelt. He put the van into gear and smiled to himself.

"What's so funny?" Miranda demanded, feeling uneasy. Did he think she was overdressed or looked silly or what?

"You are," he said, and seemed to fight back another smile.

"Well, am I dressed wrong or what?" she asked, hurt. "Why didn't you tell me?"

"You look—like a million new dollars," he muttered. "But you sure as Sam Hill don't look like a woman with a purse full of live squirrels."

She stared at him in surprise. He'd actually complimented her. "I thought you'd prefer a woman with a purse full of squirrels," she said, trying to sound airy and careless.

He shrugged again. He'd never given the matter any thought. Now that he did, he was disturbed to realize that if the heavens opened up and his ideal woman walked down to him on a staircase of sunbeams, he suddenly imagined her looking very much like Miranda, all in white and gold with her purse full of squirrels.

THEIR FIRST STOP was the hospital. Miranda's nerves danced in foreboding. She hadn't seen Duke Wilcox since she was a child, and she realized she still carried a child's fear of him.

Quint sensed her uneasiness. With atypical concern he put his hand beneath her elbow. "You all right?" he asked. "Or you one of those people scared of hospitals? It's okay."

His touch, his curt offer of moral support filled her with a giddy gratitude. But she didn't want him to see her fear. It seemed important she not show him weakness. "I'm fine," she managed to say. But her nervousness affected her stomach, and again, without thinking, she pressed her hand against her midriff.

Duke had a private room, practically smothered in flowers. He lay in bed, so massive that he seemed to have been placed, by some perverse joke, in a bed meant for a child. His tight red curls were graying, his bulldog's face was more crumpled and wrinkled, but she saw with a start that years and even serious injury hadn't lessened Duke's vital force.

He greeted Quint with a nod, then looked at Miranda so hard and so seriously that she felt he was studying her. "Dog my cats," he said in a loud voice. "You just went and got prettier, didn't you? Come here and sit by me, you li'l old troublemaker."

His face split into a wide grin. "Pull her up a chair, Quint," he said, "so's I can see her without gettin' a crick in my neck. They got so many chains and pulleys on me, I feel like one of those marionette puppets or something. Well, well, Miss Miranda Mason. You remember old Duke?"

Quint placed a chair close to Duke's bed and held it for Miranda. She sank into it, her knees slightly weak. "Yes, sir," she said with unnatural timorousness. "I remember."

"Never saw a child so bent on bein' friendly," Duke told Quint, still grinning. "No matter what her daddy said. Little bitty thing, and she was bound and determined to make friends with everybody in Cambasia. And her daddy was just as determined to keep her locked in the house. I spent more time chasin' after this child than the rest of the family put together. You remember that, Miranda?"

"I remember you catching me," she replied unhappily. She couldn't understand why Duke Wilcox seemed so pleased to see her.

He laughed again. Quint leaned against the hospital dresser, arms crossed, watching his father carefully. "How you feeling, Pop?"

"Bored!" thundered Duke. "Bored smack out of my mind! And they want to keep me here another month! Every sawbones in the Southwest wants to poke this leg. I don't like them, I don't like this place, and I don't like the food. So let me enjoy lookin' at Miranda. He treatin' you all right, honey?''

Duke rolled his pale blue eyes in her direction, and Miranda nodded nervously. She was still nonplussed by Duke—he was as large and loud as ever, but his friendliness amazed her. He seemed truly delighted to see her.

He reached over and took her hand in his own great freckled one. He squeezed it. He looked at Quint, grinning sheepishly. "This little gal," he said with pride, "was one of the most fearless children I ever did see. Her daddy said she wasn't to play with the gardener's two little boys— though they was as nice as could be. Old Miranda here would strut out the back door and go down and play with them anyhow. Only way I ever got this child back where her daddy wanted her was to jump her, screaming blue murder, like they teach you in commando school. Even that hardly fazed her. Had a mind of her own, she did."

He had actually *liked* her, Miranda thought in surprise. She couldn't have been more amazed. "You fazed me," she said, finding her courage at last. "You scared me to pieces. You could yell louder than anybody I ever heard."

"Hell's bells," shouted Duke, "I had to! It was your daddy's orders to keep you in, and the only way I could do it was by yellin' like a banshee. If you were scared, you didn't show it. Before I knew it, you'd be sneakin' off again! Oh, you were a handful, but I always thought if I had a daughter, I'd take one like you—some spirit to her."

Miranda was recovering her old boldness. "You must be strange," she teased. "Everybody said I was an awful child. Most people want daughters like Jaqueline."

"I never thought you were awful," Duke snorted. "Buford didn't neither. You drove him nuts, always gettin' stuck in trees and catchin' lizards and tryin' to raise toads in the bathtub, but he didn't think you were awful. As for Jaqueline, a prissier little prig I never saw. Walked around like she was weaned on vinegar. You were different as night and day, you two.''

Miranda smiled slightly, although she felt guilty being amused at Jaqueline's expense. Still, it felt novel and pleasant, for once, to be favorably compared to her sister. She looked at the big man in the hospital bed and realized her childhood impressions of him had been mistaken. He had been fond of her. And she realized she could be fond in turn of this vital, larger-than-life and totally honest character.

"You!" Duke bellowed at Quint. Quint looked at him mildly. "I've been thinkin'. It's time to build a better house down there on the Flirtation. You must be trippin' all over each other in that cabin.''

Quint shifted his position, as if the thought that they'd been living in such tight quarters made him uncomfortable. "We do all right," he said laconically.

"I don't care," Duke asserted. "I'm almost retired. Maybe this leg will retire me early. Suppose I want to come spend time on the river? Am I supposed to be all scootched up in that place? No sir. I'm callin' the construction company. Time to put a decent house on that river. You show Miranda the plans?''

Quint shook his head, looking as if the whole conversation rankled.

Duke turned to Miranda. "Designed it himself," he said, jerking a thumb in Quint's direction. "Did an amazin' job. Beautiful house. Plumb beautiful. And plans for expandin' the animal facilities. Got more than one talent, this one.''

Quint crossed his arms more firmly and stared out the window in chagrin.

"He's modest, too," Duke continued with affectionate malice. "Oh, don't worry, Miranda, if anybody can take care of you, this man can. Has that worthless daddy of yours found out yet who's pesterin' you with those letters?''

"No," Miranda answered. "Buford would have called me."

"Well, till then, Quint'll take care of you. Don't care if I do brag on my own. He's been tried by fire. Tried by fire and survived. You can depend on him."

"Pop—" Quint objected in frustration.

"I depend on him," Duke continued smoothly, patting Miranda's hand. "Depend on both my sons. Man couldn't ask for better sons. Know they'd do anything for me—'specially now that I'm laid up like this."

"Pop—" Quint said again, a note of warning in his voice.

"So I *know*," Duke said, staring at the ceiling as if thanking heaven for his peerless sons, "that Quint won't mind hostin' the wildlife refuge's board members' dinner this year. Jerry's got to go to Atlanta that week—it can't be helped. You'll have to do it, Quinton."

Quint's dark blue eyes flashed disbelief. "Hey," he said, suddenly wary and full of coiled energy. "Wait. No. I hate that stuff."

Duke's jaw set and his face began to flush dangerously. "No? No? I'm lyin' here on this bed of excruciatin' pain, I, your very own daddy, and you stand there and tell me no? Boy, I know your social skills leave much to be desired, but don't tell me no. You can do anything you set your mind to. What's more, you've got to. There's nobody else."

"No," Quint said stolidly, his face as determined as his father's. "I hate parties. Don't know how to give one. I'd rather stay home and floss the alligator's teeth."

Duke glowered. "It's your duty to help me in these days of my extremity."

"I can't," Quint said with elaborately clear enunciation. "I don't know how."

"Hmmph!" sneered Duke, as if he'd never heard anything so shameful in his life. He turned to Miranda. "Bet you can give a party, can't you, honey?"

"Well," Miranda said, nervous at being caught between the two of them, "I suppose." Actually, she knew she could. She'd seen Jaqueline plan hundreds of parties, and Miranda was always a member of the social committees in college.

"There!" said Duke triumphantly. "See? She'll help—she's seen this kind of stuff all her life. She'll sail right through it. You'll do a fine job."

"But—" Quint threw Miranda a hot and angry look that told her clearly she had committed the ultimate betrayal. She blushed, biting her lower lip and looking away. Duke Wilcox kept his hold on her hand. He patted it again.

"Now," he said, smoothly switching the subject so he could ignore Quint's smoldering look, "tell me about my old friend Buford. Is he still psychoanalyzing everybody?"

After talking to her for almost twenty minutes, Duke asked Miranda if she'd mind if he talked alone to his son for a few moments. She said of course she wouldn't, then rose. She told Quint she would meet him outside; it was time to feed the squirrels. Quint warned her not to talk to anyone else and she took off in a swirl of white and gold.

Duke waited until the door closed behind her. He gave Quint his sternest and most ferocious look.

"You stayin' true to your word?" he demanded. "You keepin' your distance from her? I promised her people she'd be safe with you."

"I'm keeping my distance," Quint muttered wearily. Good Lord, he thought, how had he ever got into this mess?

"Don't touch that girl," Duke said stonily. "Don't even think about it."

"Don't have time to think about it," Quint countered, his face hard. "Too busy." It occurred to him, to his complete dismay, that he thought about her all the time.

"Good," said his father, crossing his muscular arms. "That girl's had a hard enough time. She doesn't need to be hurt any more. So see that you don't."

Quint waited a moment in expectant silence. "How's she been hurt?" he asked at last.

"That idiot father of hers," Duke said in disgust. "He blamed her for something that was never her fault. Fortunately he hasn't broken her spirit." He paused, allowing himself a small smile of satisfaction. "I didn't think he could. Was she a pistol! Something special, that one."

Again the silence fell between them. "She seem happy enough out there with you?" Duke asked. "At the river?"

"She's done better than I thought," Quint admitted moodily.

Duke watched his son carefully. "I want you to be kind to her," he said very quietly. "You understand me? You take care of her like she was your own."

My own, Quint thought, and the words hit him in the pit of his stomach. But he was expert at hiding his emotions; he had been for years. "She's safe with me," he said. But those words, so easily said, seemed more mysterious and complex than any he had ever uttered. He was beginning to understand she wasn't safe at all with him.

HE FOUND Miranda outside the hospital, standing against a railing. Behind her a rosy bank of azaleas bloomed with almost supernatural beauty. A balmy spring breeze made her full white skirt billow gracefully, and tossed tendrils of her blond hair. She was feeding one of the squirrels and smiling quietly down at it.

When she looked up and saw him, again she felt as if she'd been jolted. The way he stood there staring at her flooded her with emotions she was afraid to try to understand.

Then he walked toward her, slowly, not taking his eyes from her. She could say nothing, only drink him in. Then in confusion she turned her face back to the tiny squirrel and tried to concentrate on feeding it.

He stood beside her. He leaned against the railing, still watching her. She kept her eyes on the squirrel.

"I really hate parties," he said at last, his tone gruff.

"We'll do fine," she said.

When she dared to glance up at him, he was still staring at her in that disturbing way.

"Really," she said nervously. "We'll do fine."

"Maybe." His voice was meditative.

He watched the way tendrils of her hair fluttered, golden in the breeze. He had a sudden irrational urge to reach out and touch that gold silk. Then he would let his fingers trail down to the delicate line of her cheek, the fullness of her moist and beautiful mouth.

His face went grimmer than usual. He thrust both hands in his pockets and kept them there.

CHAPTER SIX

As DUSK FELL the van jolted down the road to the cabin. Miranda sighed with satisfaction. It had been wonderful to be caught up in the bustle of a city once more, wonderful to shop again—even if it had been for jeans and boots and such—and especially wonderful to eat out. Quint introduced her to the delights of southern fried chicken, Cajun rice and native wine.

Yet glorious as a day's gallivanting had been, she was glad to be back at the cabin. The river's night sounds, which had seemed sinister less than a week ago, that night were like a peaceful symphony, welcoming her return.

Boots, the collie, gamboled about both Quint and Miranda, and Bump kept nudging her with his velvety muzzle until he almost made her drop her parcels.

Inside, unpacked, she slipped into a new pair of jeans and a turquoise-and-silver knit top. She padded out of the bedroom in her beaded white moccasins, sat down at the kitchen table and fed the baby squirrels. Quint, too, had changed into his usual jeans and a black T-shirt, which emphasized the width of his shoulders. He switched on the tape deck, letting soft music fill the room.

Miranda smiled at the squirrel baby. Quint had surprisingly sophisticated tastes in music. He liked to alternate classical music with tracks from Broadway shows and sounds from the big band era. The magical harmonies of Glen Miller's "String of Pearls" pervaded the little cabin.

He stood at the stove, heating deer formula. She could feel his eyes on her again and she looked up, trying to read his impenetrable gaze. A vague but excited tremor tingled through her.

"Is something wrong?" she asked with more casualness than she felt.

He shrugged. "I should have known," he said, and gave her approximately one-eighth of a smile.

"Known what?" she challenged, still uncomfortable under his scrutiny.

He shook his head, turning back to his work. "That you wouldn't look any different in real jeans. You're just not the understated type, are you?"

"So I've been told," she replied with cool control. His words stung. She had felt great peace and contentment being back in the cabin with him. Now the happiness drained away.

"It's okay," he muttered. "I'm getting used to it. You're just never going to be ordinary, that's all."

Her spirits sank lower. She concentrated on finishing feeding Monique, then picked up Desiree. "For your information," she said crisply, "I'd adore being a nice, understated, ordinary person. However, what you see is what you get. You're not exactly Mr. Average yourself, you know."

This time he did smile, and it made her heart flip over in tumbling confusion. She wasn't sure she had really seen him smile before. She had never realized how truly handsome he was until that moment.

"Touché." He sat down and began to feed the elder of the fawns. "Incidentally, I'm going to start the fawns on hard food soon. I want you to take over then, so they don't get too attached to either one of us."

"Of course," Miranda said. She understood the consequences for wild animals who became reliant on humans for food and shelter. She realized, too, that Quint made a profession of caring for things, then letting them go. For the first time she realized this meant her, as well. He would give her shelter as long as she needed it. Then, without a qualm, he would set her free.

For a moment, the music was the only sound in the room. "Pop brought something up." Quint spoke with great deliberation. "He said that your father blamed you for something that wasn't your fault. Want to talk about it?"

She blinked in surprise. He had avoided personal conversation up until now. She didn't know whether to tell him about it or stay silent. On impulse she spoke.

"My mother," she said slowly, "wanted another child. My father didn't. The doctors told her she shouldn't try. She did. I was born, and she died. My father never got over it. I guess my sister didn't, either—really—even though she was very young."

He held the bottle higher, so the fawn could drain the last drops. "They blame you?" He gave her a glance of disbelief. "That's crazy. How could they blame you? You were a baby, for God's sake."

Miranda didn't meet his eyes. "They loved my mother. They missed her. I—I guess they couldn't help feeling the way they did."

"Doesn't that make you angry?" he demanded. Fire glinted deep in his blue eyes, but he finished feeding the first fawn, took hold of the second and offered it a fresh bottle.

"I don't know," Miranda said helplessly, shaking her head. "I suppose. Maybe that's why I acted up so much. But then, well, last year I did a lot of thinking about the way I acted. And I tried to figure out why I behaved the way I did. Because it just made Daddy and Jaqueline more unhappy. And it didn't make me happy, either. So I tried to change."

"And?" he prodded.

She shrugged unhappily. "Nobody seemed to notice. Nobody in my family, anyway. I thought I grew up a lot. Maybe I didn't. I mean, I just started keeping to myself." Her voice almost broke, and she struggled to regain her control.

Another long silence stretched between them. "Your older sister," he said at last. "What's she like? Apple of your father's eye? All that sort of stuff?"

"Jaqueline," she murmured, "thinks like Daddy, acts like Daddy, she even looks like Daddy—only very feminine, of course, and petite."

"Your father—he favors her?"

"Well, of course," Miranda said, actually shocked. "Why shouldn't he? She's smart. She's diplomatic, and absolutely levelheaded and cool-blooded all the time."

"And you're not?" he asked, raising one dark brow.

"That," Miranda said dryly, "ought to be obvious. I'm the opposite."

Quint finished feeding the second deer and shooed it away. He stood and looped his thumbs over his belt. "Opposite, eh? I guess that makes you stupid, tactless, addle-brained and hot-blooded."

She gave a short, humorless laugh. "Well, not quite that bad. But close."

He shook his head in distaste. "Families," he said between his teeth, "should help you feel good about yourself. Not sit around counting your faults."

"They don't do that," she protested, more out of loyalty than conviction. "They just lose patience. They're perfectionists. It's hard for them to understand somebody different."

"Miranda," he continued, his voice extremely quiet, "you've been here a week. You're here because something unpleasant, possibly even dangerous, is happening. How often has your father called you?"

She'd put the second squirrel back in its cage. She toyed with her bracelet and looked at the floor in shame. "Once."

"How often has your sister called?" he went on relentlessly.

"She hasn't," Miranda answered, still playing with her bracelet. "But she's got her mind on other things. She's very involved with a man. She'll probably be engaged soon. I wanted to meet him, but..."

"Your father called once—to tell you not to call. Your sister never called. Buford, on the other hand, has called three times. Do you realize what you told my father this afternoon at the hospital?"

She frowned slightly, not understanding.

"He asked you if your father had found out who'd been sending the letters," Quint said grimly. "And you said, no, because *Buford* would have called if he did. Doesn't that strike you as odd? The one person in your household who's paying any attention to you is the butler, for Pete's sake."

Miranda swallowed hard, still refusing to meet his eyes.

"I'm not trying to make you feel bad," he said quickly. "My father told me to be kind to you. I see why. But I think the kindest thing to tell you is the fact your family treats you pretty unfairly. And they're as responsible for this situation as you are."

She snapped up her head and stared at him in surprise. "What?" she managed to say.

He remained standing over her sternly, his thumbs still hooked in his belt. "I said they're just as responsible for this mess as you are. It doesn't sound as if they ever gave you much guidance—or affection. Now, when you're in trouble, they try to pretend it isn't happening. I repeat—families are supposed to love one another."

The idea that anyone other than herself had a hand in this hellish situation was so new that Miranda could hardly contemplate it. She was even more amazed to hear Quint talk so much and to use a word so emotional as *love*. Hearing it from his lips made her feel dizzy and unhappy with yearning.

"Your family," she asked, looking up at his handsome yet forbidding face. "Did they love you?"

His expression showed nothing. He nodded. "More than most people would think humanly possible," he said. "To the bitter limit."

Now what did that mean? Miranda wondered dazedly. But he shifted his shoulders in a gesture of masculine restlessness, walked to his bunk and threw himself down on it.

"My family gives me lots of things," she objected, frightened by his words. "Schooling, money, clothes, jewelry—"

"You don't understand," he snapped. He stared in frustration at the bunk above him. He wasn't used to conversations like this, and he felt he'd handled it all wrong. He wanted to tell her that she was beautiful and vibrant and full of life, and it was starting to make him sick with anger when he saw her sad or frightened. He wanted to tell her that in some crazy way, in spite of all her artificiality, she was natural. She gloried in her femininity with the same healthy vitality that a bird gloried in its song or a deer in its fleetness. But he'd never spoken to a woman that way in his life, and he wasn't going to start with this one—especially after he'd promised everyone he was keeping his intentions honorable and his thoughts and hands off her.

"I hate parties," he grumbled, abruptly changing the subject. "This one's at Pop's house. In two weeks. You'll have to plan it."

She squared her shoulders, tossed her bangs out of her eyes. Once more she tried to gather her emotions into a tidy and manageable bundle. She stood up, her chin high. "A party I can plan," she said with resignation and satire. "That's one thing I'm good for. Remember me? The party animal. Don't worry. I won't embarrass you. My days of leopard-skin suits are over."

"I didn't mean to insult you," he said moodily, wondering why she never understood him. "I meant it as a compliment—sort of."

"Thank you—sort of," she said with spirit. She moved swiftly toward the screen door and stepped outside, letting the door slam behind her. She looked wildly around for Bump. Faithful as usual, he stepped out of the shadows and began to nuzzle her shirt. She wound her arms around his neck and buried her face against its softness.

She was teeming with frustration and confusion. She didn't understand Quint; she wasn't sure it was even possible to understand him. One moment he would give her a look that made her blood smolder; the next, he was offering cryptic advice; the next, he dismissed her as a fluffy-brained little socialite and tried to pass it off as a compliment.

"Hey!" he had yelled after her when she stalked out the door. He sat up so fast he almost hit his head on the overhanging bunk. "Where are you going?" he demanded as the door slammed. Then he swore.

He knew she'd heard him and wasn't answering. What had he said? What was wrong with her? Maybe his first impression of her was right: she was spoiled, silly, temperamental, a chronic flirt who insisted on being the center of attention. He'd tried being kind, and it had done no good. She'd walked off in a huff for no reason at all.

In disgust, he pulled off his T-shirt, flung it to the floor and fell back onto his bunk. He kicked off his black boots, letting them fall with a clatter to the floor. Let her sulk and stew, he thought grimly. He'd go to sleep. She could stay out there all night. He pulled the sheet up over his bare chest.

But he kept thinking about her, and his anger kept rising. He gritted his teeth, resisting the urge to follow her outside, grab her, tell her what he really thought and shake some sense into her beautiful golden head.

No, he thought, angrier still. If he did that, if he put his hands on her, he knew he wasn't going to shake her. He was going to pull her into his arms, hold her against him as no man had ever held her before and kiss her until . . .

He swore again, rolled over and hit the wall with his fist. He'd fallen right into her snares, he thought darkly. Right after he'd vowed again that he wasn't going to touch her. Wasn't that her specialty? Driving men to distraction? Well, she was good at it—damned good. He ought to have his head examined. He'd be safer out sleeping with the alligator and the bobcat than sharing the cabin with her.

He reached up and switched off the main light. To hell with her, he thought. He'd be delighted when the Senator nabbed that fool letter-writer and summoned his impossible daughter home. He wanted his simple, sensible routine back.

Miranda, outside, stood in the moonlight, still pressing her face against Bump's warm neck. She had heard Quint call after her, but she'd refused to answer him. Then she'd heard him thrash about briefly and saw that he'd switched the central light out.

She was glad. She hoped he fell asleep immediately. She didn't want him coming after her, confusing her more. He was an impossible mixture of gentleness and coldness—who could understand him?

Yet, perversely, her heart beat hard at the thought of him standing by her in the moonlight and looking at her. She would simply turn to him and lean against him, laying her face against his chest, feeling his infinite strength. He would hold her close to him, so close that there would be no room for all the differences between them. He would not have to say a word. He would just be Quint, holding her.

But he did not come to her. She walked slowly to the riverbank and stood, her arm around Bump's neck. Together they stared out at the spring stars and their reflections dancing on the surface of the river.

It was a long time before she returned to the cabin.

MIRANDA AWOKE with a clear memory of the previous night's confusion and unhappiness. She didn't want to think about it. She would forget, she vowed, by keeping busy; it was an old ploy, but one that almost always worked.

Quint, as usual, had arisen before her. She heard him out fussing and cussing with the alligator, Albert. Albert was a surly and difficult patient. He refused to eat, and Quint had to force-feed him every morning. It was a sight that racked Miranda's nerves: Quint matching wills with a five-foot alligator, forcing the beast's formidable jaws open and thrusting fish down Albert's unwelcoming gullet.

From the look of the kitchen, Quint hadn't bothered to breakfast. She put on a khaki shorts-and-shirt set, fed the squirrels, then set out to cook breakfast before he returned and had a chance. She started frying bacon and mixing scrambled eggs. She couldn't do any worse than he did.

He came in at last, shirtless and breathing hard from his encounter with Albert. Harry McIver had sent an injured hawk over with his son, and Quint had to try to get food down that terrified animal, as well. It was badly wing-shot and he was worried about its chances of recovery. He suspected Slayton, the poacher, had struck again.

"What are you doing now?" he asked suspiciously, watching Miranda butter toast.

"Cooking," she said shortly.

"You said you couldn't," he accused.

"I can't," she tossed back. "Which doesn't mean I can't do better than you. I either learn to do it or you'll have to start force-feeding me, too."

He grumbled something but he sat down. He ate wordlessly, shooting dark glances at her. But he took seconds and then thirds, and Miranda felt strangely triumphant. For her part, it was the first decent breakfast she'd had in days. Maybe she had a knack for this.

"Well?" she asked when he pushed back from the table at last.

His look was no more friendly than before. "Okay," he said without warmth. "You cook. It'll give me more time with the animals."

"I can still do my share with the animals," Miranda argued. "The foxes are mine. So are the raccoons. I have to take over the fawns, and I've still got the squirrels—and the ducks."

"Suit yourself," he replied tersely. "Just remember you've got a party to plan. You'll have to talk with Pop and Mrs. Petitjean. It's a big job. Twenty people for supper. It isn't eggs for two, and it isn't scraps for raccoons."

"Don't worry about me," she returned airily. "I can do it—standing on my head."

"Right." He raised his hands in mock surrender. "I forgot. The party animal."

"Right," Miranda said sweetly, clearing the table so swiftly he didn't have a chance to rise and help. "The one kind of animal you don't understand at all."

"That's because I don't deal with domestic animals," he answered.

"Why, Mr. Wilcox," she said with the same mock sweetness, "how inaccurate. I've been called many things in my life, but 'domestic' was never one of them."

He looked her up and down as she stood by the sink, plunging dishes into the sudsy water. It irritated him, but she was right. She might be in a kitchen, she might have just finished cooking breakfast, and she might be up to her elbows in dishwater, but she didn't give the impression of being at all domestic. She reminded him irrationally of Bump—a beautiful creature, wild enough to always be mysterious and just tame enough to be trouble.

He rose, shaking his head as if to clear it. "Call Pop about the party," he said shortly.

"Don't worry," Miranda assured him.

Don't worry, he thought glumly. She was a girl born to make a man worry.

"Just don't take over any more of my life," he said between his teeth.

"I very much doubt," Miranda uttered, scrubbing furiously at the dishes, "that anyone will ever take over your life. You're not exactly domesticated yourself."

He looked her up and down again. He had a brief and fiery thought about picking her up, carrying her into the bedroom and showing her just undomesticated he was. Instead, he turned on his heel and headed for the door.

MIRANDA FINISHED the dishes then began her phone calls. She would call Duke for advice on the party, and then Mrs. Petitjean to start the plans. But first she wanted to call home. Quint's remarks about her family hurt. She knew her father didn't want her to phone him, but there was nothing to prevent her from calling Jaqueline. Buford had said Jaqueline was in a flurry of activity, because her beau was back from California, but Miranda wanted to reach out to her, to make contact.

Buford answered, as usual. He said he was just putting together a bundle of mail to send her and that it all looked harmless. The Senator had a detective investigating the threatening letters, but the Senator himself was phenomenally busy. He was working fifteen hours a day, cultivating support for a bill he was introducing. He had been meeting with lobbyists every day and entertaining people of influence every night. As for Jaqueline, he said she'd been helping the Senator, but Miranda had caught her at home. And Jaqueline had important news.

He switched Miranda's call to Jaqueline's line. "Miranda?" Jaqueline asked, as if she weren't altogether pleased. "I thought you weren't supposed to call."

Miranda had hoped for a warmer welcome. "Well, Daddy said not to call him, but you know how long it takes Daddy to get over being mad—"

"Hmmph," Jaqueline said, sounding bored. "I thought maybe he was worried the phone was tapped by this—person—after you. Are you sure you should be calling?"

"Buford's phoned me," Miranda replied. "He certainly wouldn't if Daddy said it was wrong."

"Well," Jaqueline said, softening slightly. "How is it down there? You're with that Wilcox man, right? That awful marine? Where? Crabtree Corners or something? I suppose you're having fun, though. Somehow you always manage to."

"I'm not with Duke Wilcox," Miranda said, surprised. "I'm with his son. On the Flirtation River, not at Cherry Creek. Didn't Daddy or Buford tell you?"

"Not that I remember," Jaqueline answered. "Duke Wilcox's *son*? He's married, I hope."

"Er—not exactly," Miranda admitted, and hurried to safer ground. "But it's nothing to worry about. So Buford said you had big news—what is it?" she asked, changing the subject.

There was a pregnant pause. Then Jaqueline said, with great satisfaction, "Well, Miranda, I'm engaged. To Delbert. The attorney with the State Department. He wants to run for the congressional seat from Maryland next year. I think he has a fine political future—as good as Daddy's. Probably even better."

"Jaqueline!" Miranda cried with glee. "You're really engaged? How wonderful! Have you announced it? When's the date?"

"We're having a brunch next week to announce it officially. We'll be married in August."

"Next week? And the wedding's in August? Oh, Jaqueline, I had no idea things would happen so soon. And I've never even met him. Maybe I could come home—just for the brunch, to meet him."

"No!" Jaqueline said sharply. "Certainly not. You can't do that. You can't come home until this letter thing is resolved. You know that. It's upset Father terribly."

"Jaqueline," Miranda protested, "this is more important than the stupid letters. And nobody's really tried to do anything to me—just threats, that's all. I want to come home. I want to meet Delbert. This letter thing could go on clear past August. I can't stay away forever."

"Miranda," Jaqueline said coldly, "if you won't think of your own well-being, will you please think of everyone else's? We simply don't know if it's safe for you to come home—safe, I might add, for any of us. Who knows what these letters mean—they may even be a way of striking out at Father. You can't come back. Who knows what kind of jeopardy we might be in because of you? Father's just beginning to relax again—and he desperately needs to."

"Jacky, I didn't do anything," Miranda remonstrated. "I just want to see my own sister, meet my own brother-in-law-to-be—"

"Please don't call me Jacky, and please think of someone besides yourself for once," Jaqueline admonished. "You are not to return until things are cleared up. And by the way, Father's decided on a new school for you next fall."

"A new school?" Miranda wailed. "He's really going to do it? Where's he want to send me now?"

"Basel, Switzerland," Jaqueline said in her most implacable tone. "He doesn't actually think you'll do well, but some very bright young men with excellent business connections study there. You might find someone quite suitable there."

"I don't want to go to Switzerland," Miranda objected desperately. "I can't ski, I can't remember foreign verbs, and businessmen bore me."

"Miranda," Jaqueline said, "most girls would love to go to Switzerland. What's the problem? And who's this man you're staying with? Are you involved with him? Can't you go a week without some mad affair? Does Father know about this? Who is this person? What does he do? I suppose, as usual, it's something totally unacceptable."

"Daddy knows all about it," Miranda countered. "He approved. No, I'm not having a mad affair. I've never had a mad affair in my life. This man is highly honorable. He's intelligent and idealistic and dedicated. He's his own man and runs a—a philanthropic enterprise, and his family's prominent in the state. There's not one thing about him that Daddy, or anybody else, could possibly disapprove of."

"My," Jaqueline murmured sweetly, "he's certainly made an impression on you. You sound absolutely smitten."

"I am not," Miranda denied, "and don't you dare tell Daddy I am because it's not true."

"Miranda—really—are you ever going to grow up?" Jaqueline sounded irritable. "Listen—I can't talk any longer. I have important duties to tend to. Just sit tight and act like an adult, can't you? Do *not* come up here, do *not* fight Father about Switzerland, and for heaven's sake, don't fall in love with some hillbilly just because he's the only man in sight. I worry about you, Miranda. Honestly, you make me worry myself sick. Can't you please behave?"

Jaqueline hung up.

Miranda slammed down the receiver, then held her head in her hands. "I do behave!" she protested. "I am behaving! What did I ever do, really, that was so awful?"

Quint's words about her family's lack of support echoed ominously in her mind. She shook her head. She tried not to think of Jaqueline or her father.

She made her other calls. It was a pleasure to talk to Duke Wilcox, who sounded genuinely glad to hear from her. He gave her dozens of instructions for the board dinner, including the difficult order of getting Quint into a black tie and tuxedo.

She called Mrs. Petitjean, who sounded nervous and resentful. Miranda, however, had spent a lifetime talking servants into a better mood. Dealing with Mrs. Petitjean, after all the years with Buford, seemed almost easy.

She rechecked her voluminous notes, then called the recommended caterers and florists. Having done all she could for one day, she rose and went out into the bright afternoon sunshine. Harry McIver had sent over three orphaned mallard ducklings with the hawk, and she had undertaken their feeding.

She saw Quint and stopped, her hands in the pockets of her shorts. Lately when she caught sight of him a strange wave of excitement shot through her, but never so much as when he was working with Jupiter, the eagle.

Quint stood in the clearing, his shirt off and tied by the sleeves around his waist. The sun glinted on the bronzed sinews of his chest and arms. He wore one large leather gauntlet.

He was teaching the eagle to fly again as if he were training a falcon. The great bird sat on the gauntleted hand. A jess was secured on its leg and a thirty-foot nylon cord was tied to the ring on the jess. With one hand Quint swung a lure far above his head. Then, suddenly, the eagle lifted with a short, harsh cry and flew up, its great wings beating.

After Jupiter had seized his prize, Quint expertly drew the bird back to him. Miranda held her breath. Her throat felt choked with awe and love.

Love, she thought, coming to herself with a start. She hardly knew this man, and he did not want to be known, by her or anyone else. She bit her lip, remembering how she had described him to Jaqueline—as if he were some sort of god. Could it be she loved this man?

She colored with shame but still couldn't take her gaze from Quint, so tall in the clearing, the huge eagle statuesque upon his arm. Jaqueline was probably right as usual. Miranda had no doubt convinced herself she was falling in love only to cause trouble, stir things up in the family.

She tore her gaze away and pushed her hands more deeply into her pockets. She really was a fool, she thought, to have those kinds of feeling for this man—this man who could barely tolerate her. He would be appalled if he knew she thought of him in such a way.

Well, she thought stoically, she'd just stay out of his way. She'd tend the smaller animals and cook; she'd stay in touch with Duke, arrange his party and help to give it. As for Quint, she would keep her distance. If she guarded her movements carefully, they hardly had to be together except at mealtimes. They didn't have to talk. Her father had taught her long ago that just because people lived in the same house, it didn't mean they had to communicate.

She tossed her head purposefully. She'd stay as far from him as possible. It was an excellent vow, she decided, and one she intended to keep. But that was before the rains started, and the very forces of nature seemed to be conspiring to fling her and Quint together.

The clouds began forming that afternoon. Storms were brewing. They were of the most primitive sort.

CHAPTER SEVEN

THE STORM BROKE with unexpected quickness late that afternoon. It was as if the sky ripped, cascading sheets of water to the surprised earth.

"The dam has burst! The dam has burst!" screamed Ratso the crow, flapping toward the shelter of the trees. He had been teasing the ducklings, to whom he had taken an immediate jealous dislike. Miranda gathered up the downy babies because they seemed frightened by the downpour. Ducks afraid of water? she wondered with irony. But she supposed that's what happened when they had no mother to teach and shelter them.

She put them into their nest, which was well shielded from the rain. Then she locked the door of their pen and raced toward the cabin, whooping as she tried to outrace the cold rain. She was icy and drenched. Bump followed her and tried to butt his way into the house. Laughing, she pushed him back outside.

She ran to the bathroom, snatching up towels. She draped one over her dripping hair, used the other to dry the puddles she'd brought inside. Dashing to the door, where the largest puddle had formed, she ran directly into Quint. She hit the hardness of his bare, wet chest as if it had been a wall.

She reeled backward from the impact, and his hands sprang out, seizing her arms to steady her. She looked up at him. The rain had drenched his hair. It hung dark and slightly waving over his forehead. Drops of water glinted on his black lashes. His face and torso gleamed sleekly with the rain.

"Whoa," he said, still holding her. Whoa indeed, she thought. Her body felt split in two. The outer part was chilled and shivery with the rain, but within she was almost feverishly agitated. She felt his eyes studying her with an almost galvanic force, watching the tendrils of her wet hair curling from beneath the towel and the way the rain made her clothes cling to the ripe curves of her body.

He stared at her, as if strong emotions warred within him. Quickly he dropped his warm hands from her arms. Whatever his feelings had been, Miranda realized, he had taken control of them.

He stepped away, took a clean towel from a cupboard and began to vigorously dry his hair, face and chest. "Watch it," he warned her calmly. "This place is small. Walk, don't run, or we'll knock each other down."

She nodded self-consciously. Pretending to towel her hair dry, she watched him from the corner of her eye. He was donning a slicker and slipping a waterproof cover onto his oldest Stetson. "You're not going back out?" she asked. "It's a deluge."

He shrugged mildly. "Noah worked a bigger deluge than this. And he had pretty much the same job. I want to check the drainage in those pens, see how tight the shelters are." He went back out, leaving her alone.

Miranda looked after him. The rain thundered down as if it did intend to keep pounding for forty days and forty nights. She swallowed hard. The tiny space would be a more cramped and intimate shelter than any ark. The pair of fawns and the pair of squirrels—and the pair of human beings—took on a new and ominous significance.

So Miranda, who couldn't be still for long, found another slicker and went outside to work beside Quint. At first he protested curtly. But when he saw the determination shining in her gray-green eyes, he let her stay.

"Could we be flooded?" she asked, helping him prop a sagging section of fence so he could reinforce it.

He threw her a glance heavy with meaning. "We never have been."

"But that doesn't mean we couldn't?" she prodded, wiping back a wet strand of hair from her eyes. "I mean, what would happen to the animals if the river floods?"

He finished hammering a nail. Her question bothered him. She hadn't asked what would happen to her. She was worried about the animals.

"I've got a few old shelters higher up in the forest. I could put up more if I had to. Get them to higher ground."

"How?" she demanded, worried. "How would you get them all moved? Is there a road?"

"Not really," he said. He took off his hat and set it on her head, even though it was too big for her. It made her look oddly vulnerable. "If I have to, I'll carry them up."

"On your back, I suppose," she said with a tinge of sarcasm, although she had no doubt he would do exactly that.

"If I have to."

She imagined him with a half-grown deer slung across his shoulders, slogging up the mountain through the rain. She knew he would do anything he had to for the animals, and he was strong enough to succeed. It was at that moment, standing drenched and cold in the rain, his too-large hat perched on her head, that she knew she loved him. It was no silly schoolgirl crush; it was love. It was also hopeless. She would never let him know what she felt. Disguising her feelings wouldn't be hard. She'd disguised the pain of rejection all her life.

"I'd put another nail there," she said, gesturing at the fence post.

"Don't," he said with a sideways glance at her, "get bossy on top of everything else." But he hammered in another nail.

THAT NIGHT Miranda made hot chocolate after supper. She sat at the table trying unsuccessfully to repair her fingernails, a task that was proving futile. Quint sat across from her, frowning above a sheet of paper. He wore a black sweatshirt, the sleeves pushed up, revealing his powerful forearms. He wrote brief sentences, then frowned harder and crossed them out.

"What are you doing?" Miranda demanded.

"Writing."

"I can see that," she said in frustration. "*What* are you writing?"

He threw down his pen. "Why don't you keep curling your cuticles or whatever it is you do?"

"Don't worry about my manicure," she retorted. "When I do your old party, I'll put on false nails. I know, it's superficial, but that's my specialty—being superficial. So what are you writing?"

"Words," he said. "A letter."

"Hmm," murmured Miranda, tapping the paper with her emery board. "You don't seem to be doing such a good job. It must be a letter in which you have to pretend to be pleasant."

The look she gave him was so sassy and impish he couldn't fight back one of his maddening half smiles.

"What is it?" she pursued. "A love letter?"

"I don't," he said with strong distaste, "write love letters."

No, Miranda thought grimly, *I'll bet you don't.*

The thought hurt. She pushed it away. "Then what kind of letter are you *trying* to write?" she asked, all arch impertinence again.

"Fund-raising," he said darkly.

"Fund-raising?" she asked in true surprise. "Is that all?"

"What do you mean, 'Is that all'?" he practically sneered. "Did you ever have to write a letter to a bunch of strangers asking for a couple of million dollars?"

"Sure," Miranda countered calmly, resting her chin on her hand. "For Daddy's campaign funds. It's one of the few things Jaqueline would rather have me do. She says she doesn't have my shameless streak. I've worked with Daddy's election committee a couple of times. I love writing to strangers for money. It's easy."

"Easy," he mocked.

"Sure," Miranda said. "What are you raising funds for?"

"You're such a nosy woman," Quint muttered. "I'm supposed to help raise money for the Wilderness Conservancy, if you have to know."

"Oh," Miranda replied, musing. "Them. I've heard of them. Good group. It'd be child's play to write for them."

He stared at her. She was, as usual, full of surprises. Few people knew of the Wilderness Conservancy. It was a private environmental group that kept a low profile. It worked to save wilderness areas on one single, brilliant principle. It bought them. It had already saved more than two million acres from development and, in the process, protected almost a thousand species of threatened plants and animals.

"Child's play, eh?" he asked sardonically.

"Piece of cake," Miranda returned confidently.

"Piece of cake," he repeated, his sarcasm even more edged. Without another word he picked up the tablet and

FREE BOOKS!

FREE GIFTS!

PLAY THE "LUCKY 7" SLOT MACHINE GAME!

AND YOU COULD GET FREE BOOKS, A FREE PEN AND WATCH SET AND A SURPRISE GIFT!

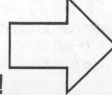

NO COST! NO OBLIGATION!
NO PURCHASE NECESSARY!

PLAY "LUCKY 7"
AND GET AS MANY AS SIX FREE GIFTS...

HOW TO PLAY:

1. With a coin, carefully scratch off the three silver boxes at the right. This makes you eligible to receive one or more free books, and possibly other gifts, depending on what is revealed beneath the scratch-off area.

2. You'll receive brand-new Harlequin Romance® novels, never before published. When you return this card, we'll send you the books and gifts you qualify for absolutely free!

3. And, a month later, we'll send you 8 additional novels to read and enjoy. If you decide to keep them, you'll pay only $1.99 per book, a savings of 26¢ per book. There is no extra charge for postage and handling. There are no hidden extras.

4. We'll also send you additional free gifts from time to time, as well as our newsletter.

5. You must be completely satisfied, or you may return a shipment of books and cancel at any time.

FREE—digital watch and matching pen

You'll love your new LCD quartz digital watch with its genuine leather strap. And the slim matching pen is perfect for writing that special person. Both are yours FREE as our gift of love.

PLAY "LUCKY 7"

Just scratch off the three silver boxes with a coin.
Then check below to see which gifts you get.

YES! I have scratched off the silver boxes. Please send me all the gifts for which I qualify. I understand I am under no obligation to purchase any books, as explained on the opposite page.

118 CIH FAUY

NAME

ADDRESS   APT

CITY   STATE   ZIP

 WORTH FOUR FREE BOOKS, FREE PEN AND WATCH SET AND FREE SURPRISE GIFT.

 WORTH FOUR FREE BOOKS AND FREE PEN AND WATCH SET

 WORTH FOUR FREE BOOKS

 WORTH TWO FREE BOOKS

DETACH AND MAIL CARD TODAY

HARLEQUIN "NO RISK" GUARANTEE
- You're not required to buy a single book—ever!
- You must be completely satisfied or you may return a shipment of books and cancel at any time.
- The free books and gifts you receive from this "Lucky 7" offer remain yours to keep in any case.

If offer card is missing, write to:
Harlequin Reader Service, 901 Fuhrmann Blvd., P.O. Box 1867, NY 14269-1867

pen and handed them to her with false courtliness. "Okay, blondie. Give me a piece of cake."

Miranda tossed her hair. "No problem. Just don't call me blondie. I hate nicknames."

"I'll remember that." He rose and went to his bunk stretching out with the latest issue of a zoological journal.

Miranda's fingers burned where his had brushed hers. Although she was acting with typical bravado, she was altogether too conscious of his long form stretched out on the bed. He had more animal magnetism than all of his animals combined. When the thunder rumbled in the dark sky, it was as if it echoed the tumble of confusion and longing within her.

But she bent her head and began to write madly. As usual, she would escape her emotions by taking action, any action. She paused from time to time to ask him questions, which he answered brusquely. She worked feverishly for an hour and a half. Then she told him she was finished.

Slowly he rose and came to stand behind her. In silence he read over her shoulder.

"Um" was all he said.

"Well?" Miranda asked, suddenly anxious for his approval. She turned to look up at him. His eyes were still on the pages. "What do you think?"

"Two things." He kept his gaze on the papers. "First, you're probably the worst speller in the world."

Miranda's heart sank. "Tell me something I don't know," she said glumly.

"Second," he said, "that's probably the best letter for the organization I've ever seen. It's great."

"Great?" she asked in pleased disbelief. "Did you say *great*?"

Almost too casually he put one hand on her shoulder and caressed it lightly. "Great. You can do it all, can't you? No wonder all the men fall in love with you."

At his touch, Miranda almost went faint. She wanted nothing more than to lay her hand upon his, to keep his strong fingers touching her. But she only sat, still as a stone. He never looked at her. But she saw a vein jump in his temple, a muscle in his jaw jerk. Immediately he removed his hand. He jammed it in his back pocket as if it had offended him and must be exiled.

"You must have driven your English professors crazy," he said gruffly. "You write beautifully, but you can hardly spell."

"Jaqueline's the family speller," Miranda said softly. It was all she could think of to say.

Apparently he could think of nothing to say himself. At last he muttered, "It's a good letter. Thanks." She nodded, not trusting herself to speak.

Miranda did not sleep well that night. Quint did not, either. She lay awake in bed unaware that he spent a long time standing by the window in the darkened main room, listening to the drumming of the rain. It was pounding hard and strong as the blood in his veins. He flexed his right hand carefully, remembering the feel of her warmth, the way her hair had brushed against his fingers like silk.

He remembered a line from an old song and winced. He stared harder into the stormy night. The line from the song ran through his head again. He cursed himself for being haunted by it. It was the simplest of lines: "I've grown accustomed to her face."

DAY AFTER DAY the rain beat down. Miranda had seen such rains in both Cambasia and India, but never before had she felt so trapped by them. The phone lines held. Each day she talked to Duke and Mrs. Petitjean, refining the plans for the party. It seemed strange to be planning an elegant party when she and Quint were in such a primitive setting, just trying to deal with the elemental force of the storm.

But she forged ahead. It was a strange existence but satisfying. One minute she'd be calling the finest wine cellar. The next she might be crouched in the rain beside Quint as he force-fed the alligator. He was lacing its fish with antibiotics now; the animal was growing sicker. Quint worried that he would lose it, and Miranda didn't even wonder why one of the most important questions in her life was whether a wounded alligator named Albert would survive.

Buford called faithfully every other day. He was kind and commiserated with her that she was probably going to miss Jaqueline's wedding. Another threatening letter had arrived at the house, and the writer said he knew Miranda was gone, but he would find her. The letter irritated Buford, but he told Miranda not to be concerned. The writer, he was convinced, was a coward, more interested in frightening her than actually hurting her.

Buford's closing words were always sterner, however, and conveyed the message that she shouldn't get herself involved with Quint. "Your daddy thinks you might flirt up to him on purpose, thinking you'll get to go somewhere else. And your daddy says that better not happen, you've got yourself in enough trouble already."

"Tell Daddy not to worry," Miranda always replied. "This man couldn't be less interested in me." Then she would add perhaps the finest defensive lie she had ever told. "Nor could I be less interested in him," she'd sniff. "He's always putting methiolate on a skunk or something. Hardly my style, Buford."

"How do you know what your style is?" Buford challenged. "You spent so much of your life pretending, you haven't a notion of what your style is."

"Piffle and double piffle," Miranda said.

"Don't you go 'piffle' at me," Buford countered. "I've known you too long. You behave, hear me?"

"I am behaving," she insisted. *But not by choice,* she thought gloomily.

She tried to call Jaqueline but could seldom reach her. When she did get through, she became more and more aware for the first time in her life that Jaqueline, beneath her alternating moods of sternness and sweetness, could be snide. "I hope you still don't think you're mad about that mountain man," Jaqueline said, smugness clear in her voice. "Father would be livid if he thought you'd sink that low. So please don't do it just to spite him. I can't imagine anything that would make his life harder. Behave yourself, Miranda."

"I am behaving," Miranda replied, practically weeping with frustration. "If I was behaving any better the boredom would kill me! And, Jaqueline, I want to come home for the wedding. I really do."

"It's impossible," Jaqueline said stonily. "Buford must have told you those letters are coming again. You have to stay where you are. For Father's good. For your own good. For everybody's good. Can't you understand that?"

"I understand," Miranda answered. But she was starting o want to go home badly. Not because she was homesick. 3he was lovesick. Being so near Quint, day in, day out, was such a complex combination of pleasure and anguish, her whole body ached.

As for Quint, a sense of trouble gnawed him. He talked to his father daily, sometimes more. Duke was getting bet-er, but one message never changed. "Keep your hands off that girl. I gave my promise she'd be safe with you, and if I can't trust you, I might as well go back and let the truck fall on me good and finish me off. Don't touch her, hear me?"

"I gave my word," Quint would say between his teeth. "Have I ever broken it?"

"No," Duke would admit. After a moment of tense silence, he would add, "And see that you damn don't break it."

After Quint hung up the phone, he would stare at it as if he could melt it by the power of his resentment. It would be simpler if he merely desired the girl. But he had grown fond of her, too fond, and he was not a man who wanted such feelings. They made him angry.

The rain, too, disturbed him. It was bad enough that it forced him into more physical closeness with Miranda than he could bear, but he had never seen such torrents. The Flirtation had never, in recorded history, flooded as high as the cabin and animal shelters, but he was worried. He knew how difficult it would be getting all the animals to higher ground.

He imagined wrestling them up through the woods in the raging rain and frowned unhappily. And he knew he wouldn't be doing it alone. Nothing he could say would keep Miranda from trying to help, even if she killed herself doing it.

Not only was he concerned about the animals, he was worried about Miranda. It wasn't that the flood could hurt her; he knew he could protect her from that. He was plagued by other worries about her. He wondered who was sending her the letters and why. She never talked about them, as if she accepted them as some terrible fate she deserved. She didn't even question her father's coldness about the whole business.

Instead, she threw herself into everything so hard he feared she was wearing herself out. She had caught cold, and often she had no appetite. She seemed uncharacteristically unhappy and moody, and sometimes he would see her unconsciously put her slender hand on her midsection as if she were in pain. As vital and vibrant as she was, he was certain she wasn't as healthy as she appeared.

He decided to make his move without letting her know ahead of time. He told her he wanted to get into the nearest town for supplies before the roads got worse. But he'd also made a doctor's appointment for her.

She'd been excited, like a happy child, when he told her they were going to town. She wanted to buy a cookbook, since she'd been doing all the cooking by instinct, and she was also eager to buy a few utensils.

But when he pulled up in front of the doctor's office, she rebelled, and he found for the first time in their ever-prickly relationship that they were having an out-and-out fight.

Miranda was furious that he had made the appointment without asking her. She insisted she wasn't sick.

"The hell you aren't," he countered. They were sitting in the van, and rain blurred the windows. "You've got a cold. And you look exhausted."

I am exhausted, she thought miserably. *I'm worn-out trying not to love you and tired to death of trying not to show you that I love you.*

Instead she said, "A cold's nothing—and who wouldn't be exhausted, putting up with you all the time?"

"There's more," he snapped. "Something's wrong with you. Don't lie to me. I can tell by the way you hold your stomach sometimes." He pressed his hand against his, showing her what he meant.

Miranda flinched slightly. He'd noticed. But what did he think? Her eyes widened, then suddenly narrowed. "What's the matter?'' she asked bitterly. "Do you think I'm pregnant? That my father sent me down here to have an illegitimate baby? And foisted me off on you? Is that it?''

Under the brim of his Stetson, his deep-set blue eyes took fire. "I never said that.''

"Well, it's probably what you think,'' Miranda shot back, nearly in tears. "I know what you think of me. You've made that clear from the first. But it just so happens I'm not pregnant. What's more I couldn't be, because I've never—''

She cut herself off. He'd never believe she was a virgin. Nobody ever did.

"I don't think you're pregnant,'' he said between his teeth. It drove him half-crazy the way she could make him as angry as she did. "I know a thing or two about biology, blondie. You don't act pregnant. You act in pain.''

"Since when do you have a licence to diagnose humans?'' she snapped back. "Why don't you stick to your—your raccoons and leave me alone?''

"Because,'' he said, the muscle in his jaw starting to jerk dangerously hard, "you may fool everybody else, but you don't fool me. Come on.''

His patience gone, he grabbed her by the wrist, opened his door and practically pulled her from the van. His grip on her wrist hurt, and she tried to push him away. "I'm not going in there,'' she insisted, pushing at him again. "Let go!''

"You're going if I have to carry you,'' he nearly snarled, glaring down at her.

"You wouldn't dare—you—'' Her own eyes flashed fire.

"Watch me,'' he said with maximum grimness.

Before she had time to comprehend what he was doing, he had swept her up into his arms and was striding purposefully through the rain toward the doctor's office.

"Put me down!'' Miranda cried.

"Be quiet," he ordered.

For reasons she didn't even understand, she obeyed.

Miranda, the doctor suspected, had an ulcer. He said she might have had it since her teens. He gave her a prescription for the ulcer, some medicine for her cold and strict orders to rest and relax.

She and Quint went to the drugstore, then drove back to the cabin in the rain. Miranda had sunk into atypical silence. She slumped against the seat in dejection, feeling caught out and betrayed.

"You must have suspected something," he said at last, tossing her a cold, sidelong glance.

"I guess so," she murmured, staring at the windshield wipers. "I think I probably figured it out when I was about sixteen."

He shook his head. "Why," he asked with mock patience, "didn't you do anything?"

"Oh, I don't know," she replied unhappily. "I thought it'd go away. And the one thing Daddy always said about me was at least I was healthy. Jaqueline was the delicate one. I was strong as a horse, or was supposed to be. Surprise, folks. One more thing wrong with old Miranda."

He swore. "You thought your family would resent your being sick? And they never noticed? I can't believe these people."

Dejected, she stayed silent.

He didn't speak for a long time, either. At last he said, "There's a thermos of water under the seat. You might as well start taking your pills."

She sighed, groped for the thermos and obeyed him again. That he should demonstrate such concern for her made her want to cry. Only Buford had ever treated her that way, and Buford was the one human being in the world she suspected might truly love her a little. But Quint's interest had to be purely clinical, she told herself. She was simply another case to him, like one of the animals.

"The letters," he said after another long silence. "The threatening letters. What do they say? Exactly. Can you tell me?"

She shrugged tiredly. "They say lots of things. I can show you."

He turned and gave her a sharp look. "What?"

She shrugged again, avoiding his eyes. "I can show you. I mean, they're not obscene or anything."

"You mean you have them?" he demanded, scrutinizing her as if seeing her for the first time.

"All but the latest ones. You can look at them if you want."

He nodded slowly, then forced his gaze back to the road. "Yeah," he said at last. "I'd like to see them. I'd like that a lot."

Things were suddenly starting to make a sick kind of sense to him. "Tell me," he said carefully, "more about your family. Especially about your sister."

She told him a little, and that listlessly. He made her rest when they got back to the cabin. She didn't want to, but he finally convinced her. When he went outside he left her sitting up in the bed, propped against the pillows. She was reading her new cookbook as if it were a novel. For some reason, her being there made him feel strange, as if something within him was either dying or coming to life.

The rain poured down harder. He looked at the swollen river, calculating carefully. They were still safe; they could hold out against the river another seven or eight days. Of that he was sure.

But what he was going to do about the woman in the cabin, he wasn't sure at all.

In spite of the rain, Bump stood, a soaking, faithful sentry, outside the cabin door. The crazy deer was waiting in the downpour for Miranda because it loved her.

"Bump," he said softly, more to himself than the deer, "you're as stupid as they come to love that girl."

Ratso, who had been lurking in the shelter of the eaves, suddenly swooped down to Quint's shoulder. "Love that girl," the crow jeered. "Stupid! Stupid! Stupid!"

"Stupid," Quint repeated dourly. He stared at the relentless rain.

CHAPTER EIGHT

MIRANDA WAS not the world's best patient. Quint fought to keep her inactive. He managed to confine her to the cabin, but she defied him by cleaning the place from top to bottom.

"I told you to get in bed and stay in bed!" he thundered when he came in to find she had scrubbed the tiled floors. "And don't scrub floors, dammit! You're not the charwoman."

Miranda, in shorts and an oversized T-shirt, put her hands on her hips, tossed her hair and glared up at him in defiance.

"This floor screamed to be scrubbed," she said staunchly. "I can't stay in bed all day. Resting makes me restless. Relaxing makes me tense. I want to go out. I want to go to the cave and take a shower. You can't stop me."

Good Lord, he thought, fury and frustration rising in him. Keeping her in line was impossible. He might as well try to subdue the sunshine or give orders to a rainbow.

"Go to bed!" he roared.

"Not until I have a shower," Miranda countered. "That floor was dirty. Now so am I."

"You're not going out in that rain. If you've got to wash up, I'll bring a tub in here."

"An old tub? Like the one you use for the deer's water? No. I'm not taking a bath in an old water trough."

"Yes, you are," he said between clenched teeth. "And it won't be old. I've got a new one in the shed. You'll get in it and then go to bed like a good girl, or I get on the phone and cancel that party."

Her eyes widened in apprehension. "You wouldn't do that!" she accused. "After all our work—your father and Mrs. Petitjean and me, too—we've got everything planned!"

"As far as I'm concerned," he said, his dark blue eyes cold, "you're just like that crazy, fractious alligator. I'll do what I have to to get you well. If that means threats and baths in deer troughs, tough. And if I have to carry you into the bedroom and throw you on the bed myself, remember, you asked for it."

Miranda blinked hard and realized that they were staring at each other with great intensity. She could feel her breasts rising and falling swiftly beneath the thin, oversized shirt. It was as if his words about throwing her into bed had stripped away some thin veil that hung between them so that they stood before each other in emotional near nakedness.

Her feelings frightened her. Apprehension and desire tingled within her body. His eyes, which had been cold a moment before, now blazed hot and searing as indigo flames.

"I," he said, jerking a thumb at his chest, "am the boss here. Understand?"

She tried to slow her erratic breathing. She bit her lip, hoping he wouldn't see how deeply he stirred her emotions.

"I understand," she said at last, looking away from him in confusion.

"Good." He bit the word off.

He brought in the large tub and filled it with hot water. It sat in the middle of the main room, between the table and the bunks. Steam rose from the surface of the water.

He nodded curtly toward the tub. "Get in."

Miranda looked at him in alarm. "Not until you get out," she said righteously.

Without a word he picked up his hat and jammed it back on. "I'll be back in half an hour," he warned. "I expect to find you in bed. Or else." He turned and strode out into the rain.

Or else what? Miranda wondered with anxiety. Would he really carry her into the bedroom and throw her onto the bed? And if he did, what would happen then? Something strange and primitive was beginning to develop between them. She could feel it. He was starting to look at her with a desire he kept under strong control, but she didn't want him merely to desire her. She wanted him to love her. But he would not. He was too much his own man.

Quickly she shed her clothes and slipped into the warm water. The metal tub was large, and its crudeness made the silkiness of the warm water seem all the more sensuous.

She shampooed her hair, then stirred her favorite bath crystals into the water, so that the bubbles frothed up and covered the wet swell of her breasts with creamy suds. She soaped herself until her body felt sleek with cleanliness and perfumed scent. She had pinned her hair in a loose knot on top of her head, and damp tendrils spilled down, tickling her neck and ears.

The warmth of the bath magically drained away the nervous energy that had propelled her. She felt languid and warm and satiny. She closed her eyes, sampling the bliss of it. She imagined a world where she and Quint were not separated by impenetrable differences. A world where they could reach out and do something as simple and wonderful as merely touch.

SHE WAS jarred from her combination of daydream and true dream by the shrilling of the phone. Her eyes snapped open. The phone rang again, insistent.

Quickly Miranda scrambled from the tub. A glance at the kitchen clock told her that almost half an hour had passed. Quint would be back shortly.

Her robe was on the other side of the tub, so she simply draped the large bath towel about herself and snatched up the jangling phone. "Hello?" she said breathlessly.

"Miz Wilcox?" The pleased and polite voice belonged to Harry McIver. When he talked to her, he always sounded like a shy schoolboy. "Uh . . . is that old boy Quint there?"

Miranda glanced at the door self-consciously. She tried to pull the towel up into a more modest position. No matter how she adjusted it, though, too much rounded bosom and tanned thigh still gleamed against its whiteness.

"No, Harry, he isn't. He should be back soon. Should I have him call you?"

"Uh . . . would you do that, ma'am? Tell him I got another hawk for him. And another broke-leg fox. I'll get 'em over as soon as I can. Also, tell him that Slayton's been telephoning fish over that way. Ask him to keep an eye out."

Wondering if she'd heard correctly, Miranda stared at the receiver. "*Telephoning* fish, Harry?"

"Yes, ma'am. He'll understand. Thank you, ma'am. Don't you all get swept away by all this rain. I swear, we'll grow webs between our toes before it's over."

Miranda said goodbye. Just as she hung up the phone, a tremor of anxiety shot through her. The front door opened. She pulled her towel more tightly about her and stood as if paralyzed.

Quint halted in the doorway. He was so tall he almost filled it. His eyes did a strange slow dance, traveling up and down her body, then resting on her eyes.

He took his hat off, hung it on a hook. He did the same with his dripping slicker. He kicked off his wet boots. But not once did his eyes leave hers.

He thinks I planned this, Miranda thought in panic. She was nearly naked, still rosy and glowing from the bath. The white towel could not begin to hide her full, gleaming breasts or the long sweep of her legs. She felt guilty and foolish.

"Harry McIver just called," she said, struggling not to stammer. "He said that he has a—a hawk and a fox with a broken leg."

Quint stood watching her, one dark brow drawn down low.

"He said he'd bring them over soon."

Still he said nothing. His shoulder moved in that masculine half shrug whose meaning she never understood. The motion always seemed partly threatening.

"Why aren't you in bed?" he asked at last. The air between them almost shook with electricity.

"I told you," she said with false bravado. "Harry called. I—kind of dozed off in the tub. The phone woke me."

She moved as quickly and discreetly as she could to the other side of the tub, picked up her white terry robe and slipped into it. She let the towel fall to her feet as she pulled the robe shut and belted it tightly.

"Harry said something about Slayton," she chattered nervously. "Something strange. That you should keep an eye out because he was telephoning fish over this way."

"Miranda," Quint warned, his voice harsh.

"What's that mean?" she asked with a shaky little laugh. "How do you telephone a fish, for heaven's sake?"

His mouth took on a hard slant. "He means Slayton's either dynamiting fish or electrocuting them out of the water. Sending them a wire. Miranda—" The same warning note edged his tone when he repeated her name.

"Why would he do that?" she demanded. Quint moved toward her, but she stood her ground, pulling her belt tighter.

"It's another kind of poaching," he said tightly. "Fish don't bite when the river's roiled, so Slayton stuns them and takes all he wants."

"Not very sporting," Miranda murmured. He loomed over her now, his eyes unreadable.

"Neither are you." His gaze fell to her hands, clutching the collar of her robe as if to cover even her throat from his sight.

"What do you mean?" she asked, her heart beating hard.

"You know what I mean." The line of his jaw was dangerous. His lean hand stretched out, gathering the front of her robe. "I don't want to catch you like this again. Don't try to tempt me. Get to bed."

"I didn't try to tempt you."

Quint smiled, tight-lipped. "Yes, you did. From the start. It won't work, Miranda. I'm not one of your college boys. I don't play games."

"I'm not playing games," she managed to whisper. She could feel the heat of his fingers even through the thick fabric of her robe.

"Yes, you are," he said with the same condescending smile. "But I'm not. And I won't."

He drew his hand away from the robe slowly. He crossed his arms. "Go to bed, Miranda. Alone."

A myriad of conflicting emotions boiled within her. She felt both innocent and guilty, consumed at once by love and hate. She would die before she let him see the tears that stung from being held back. She tossed her head so the moist blond ringlets swung.

"Why on earth," she said with all the dignity she could summon, "would I want you? You're no more civilized than one of those animals out there. Don't flatter yourself. I'm not that desperate. Nor am I ever likely to be."

She wheeled and stamped barefoot into the bedroom. He stood staring after her. By dint of enormous effort he kept himself from following her and showing her that he wasn't one of her puppyish college boys and that what she was asking for was far more dangerous—and powerful—than she knew.

Instead he swore and went to the phone to call Harry McIver. "Listen, Harry," he said, running his hand restlessly through his dark hair. "Can you put more men on Slayton? I'm so sick of this guy I could break his neck."

Miranda, clad now in a long, lacy nightdress, could clearly hear the animosity in Quint's voice. Slayton's neck wasn't the only one he wanted to break. He would probably also cheerfully throttle her. She had been stupid and careless to let him catch her half-naked. It only confirmed what he had thought from the first. She was a flirt, a shallow coquette, a temptress whose price was not impressively high.

She climbed miserably under the sheet and buried her face in the pillow. She would call Jaqueline later in the day and beg her to change their father's mind. Miranda had to go home. She was sorry she'd ever seen the Flirtation River. Its very name mocked her.

The remainder of Miranda's day passed in restlessness and frustration. Her lifeline to the outside world had become the party. The highlight of each day was talking to Duke Wilcox. She wondered why as a child she had ever feared this man, for she had grown truly fond of him.

After she talked to Duke that afternoon, Buford called. He sounded distant and troubled, not his normal self. It perplexed her. As usual he told her to behave herself but would say no more, simply telling her not to worry.

In despair she called Jaqueline, who gave her more information but less sympathy.

"I want to come home," Miranda pleaded. "I can't stay here any longer."

"You can't come home," Jaqueline stated adamantly. "Those letters are coming every single day. And now they're not postmarked New York. They're from Alexandria. That means this person is practically on top of us, Miranda."

"I don't care!" Miranda protested. She didn't fear the letter writer nearly as much as she feared Quint and her emotions. "I've got to get out of here, Jaqueline—Daddy can get me a guard, a Secret Service man, I don't care. I'll do whatever he wants. I'm being left out of everything in the family. I've never even met your fiancé."

"You've seen his picture," Jaqueline said, as if that were enough.

"Yes, and he's very handsome," Miranda lied diplomatically. In actuality, Delbert was portly, balding, and reminded Miranda of a soft-boiled egg with eyebrows.

"So you said before. Over and over," Jaqueline answered. "You probably wouldn't hit it off anyway. Delbert's very serious. Not your type."

"Oh," Miranda answered impatiently, willing to poke fun at herself. "I'd like him. You know me. Any man's my type."

"That," Jaqueline replied stiffly, "is your problem, isn't it? Well, I'm not that way. I'd like to be happy with Delbert and for once in my life not wear myself out worrying about you. Please stay where you are, Miranda, or Father will just have to send you to Switzerland early. And he's so tired, Miranda. You can't imagine how hard he's been working lately. He doesn't have time for any more of your escapades."

Miranda felt shamed and selfish when she hung up. She stared glumly out at the rain. She fed the squirrels, who were becoming agile creatures with distinct personalities. They wouldn't need her much longer. They no longer required their night feedings. She felt a wave of inexpressible loneliness.

FIVE MORE tension-filled days passed. The rain had been falling for more than a week. Quint still insisted she stay inside, which made her twitchy and irritable. Her cold had disappeared and she felt fine—thanks to her medications, much better than usual.

The party was only three days away and Miranda was constantly on the phone, feverishly making plans. Yet, the party had become less important to her. She worried about other things. Quint was working longer hours than ever, pointedly avoiding her, speaking hardly at all.

She began to feel frivolous and useless. She planned a party he didn't want while he labored to set up extra emergency shelters on higher ground.

The rain rumbled down out of the sky without ceasing. The harder it rained, the harder Quint worked, and the more silent and distant he grew.

"Are we going to be flooded?" she asked him quietly that night.

He shrugged wearily. He shot her a glance of such heated scrutiny it belied his exhaustion. But he said nothing.

"Look," she said, her own weariness and frustration taking over, "do you want me to call off this stupid party? I know you don't want it. We can't leave if the river keeps rising. Should I—"

"Don't worry about the party," he said curtly.

He had more important things to occupy him—the rain, the rising river, the endangered animals and, most troubling, Miranda herself. The water was coming down too fast, too steadily. He'd never seen anything like it. If it didn't stop soon, he was going to be moving them all out. Including Miranda. And he didn't know what he was going to do with her. He couldn't have her camping in a rain-drenched tent with him up on the mountainside. He couldn't send her off, because there was nowhere to send her, and he, after all, was responsible for her. He'd given his word.

He could send her back to his father's mansion in Cherry Creek to handle the party alone. She was a capable girl, and he knew she could do it and probably with great style. But Mrs. Petitjean would be hysterical, certain that Miranda would bring danger to the house. He supposed he could hire an armed guard or two to assuage Mrs. Petitjean's hysteria. Hell, he didn't know. He'd cross that bridge when he came to it.

In the meantime, Slayton was using the confusion caused by the rain to wreak more than his usual havoc. Harry McIver said there was evidence Slayton was setting snares for animals moving to higher ground, and he was also haunting the relatively still parts of the river, dynamiting fish, a practice Quint abhorred.

Miranda sat watching him. He looked so darkly thoughtful, so pushed to his limits, her impatience with him dissolved. She suspected the rain was worse than anyone could have foreseen, and it threatened everything.

"Maybe it'll stop soon," she said at last. "The rain."

"Maybe," he answered mechanically, without conviction. One of the little fawns butted at him playfully, but he shooed it away, not wanting it to get attached to him.

"It can't go on forever," she said, trying to offer hope.

"It doesn't have to," he replied grimly. "It only has to go on another two days or so."

"What if we have to move?" she asked, as if sensing the true seriousness of the situation for the first time.

"I move us," he said simply.

"Where do you move me?" she breathed, feeling sick and bereft because she was sure she knew the answer.

"Cherry Creek," he said without emotion. "I'll get you a guard. And then maybe the best thing would be to send you where you want to go—home. It may come to the point where I can't take care of you. I've got too much else to do. You could handle the party alone, couldn't you? You're used to that sort of thing. Washington hostess and all. It should be a piece of cake, as you said."

"Oh" was all Miranda said. "Sure. It's the least I could do."

Quint, fatigued to the bone, threw himself down on his bunk in clothes that were still damp. What was he saying? he asked himself. He couldn't send her back to Georgetown. He feared that was the last place he should send her. He had thoughts about her family he didn't want to pursue, suspicions he didn't want to dwell on. He'd promised to protect her, hadn't he? On the other hand, he knew life would be one hundred percent better without Miranda.

The hell it would, he thought angrily. When he finally fell into uneasy sleep, he was haunted by dreams he hadn't had since high school. In these dreams his younger self, like Miranda, was careless and guilt-ridden, the outcast and misfit. Only his family's love had saved him. But who if not himself would save her?

Miranda waited until Quint slept. She moved quietly to the phone. She needed to call Buford and tell him she might be coming home. At least she then would be free of the chronic agony of Quint's nearness.

But Buford wasn't home. He was at his night class. Miranda finally reached Jaqueline, who sounded impatient.

"Father's having a get-together for colleagues, Miranda," she said in a chill voice. "I'm in the middle of a very important party."

"I may be coming home," Miranda said bluntly. "There's an emergency here. They—don't think they can keep me much longer. And tell Daddy I'm not going to Switzerland."

There was a beat of silence. "You can't come home," Jaqueline said, her voice suddenly more sympathetic. "I'm sorry, Miranda. Whoever's writing those letters knows all your movements. You don't dare come home. It's too dangerous."

"I've got no place else," Miranda said desperately. "Please, Jaqueline—help me. Think of something, have Daddy think of something. *Please*."

Another beat of silence. "Poor Miranda," Jaqueline said at last. "Your chickens have come home to roost, haven't they? Don't worry, dear. We'll think of something. But don't count on coming here. I really think you'd be safer out of the country. I always have. Maybe Daddy can send you to Switzerland early."

When Miranda hung up, she wanted to weep. She did not. Instead, she walked to the window and looked out at the darkness. If anything, the driving rain was worse.

SHE AWOKE with a start. The rain beat with its same crazed fury, and the first gray light of dawn barely lighted the sky.

What had awakened her? she wondered groggily, slipping from bed. She drew on her robe. Quint was up, looking resolute yet haggard. He was unshaven but fully dressed, drawing on his slicker.

"What is it?" she asked, frightened. It was still quite dark out.

"It hasn't slowed," he said tersely. "I'm going to start moving them."

"Now?"

"Now," he replied. "If it doesn't stop today, we're in trouble. I'll get as many up there as I can. Then I'll get you to Harry somehow and have him take you to Cherry Creek."

"Have Harry come help you," she begged. "And his boys. You can't do all this alone."

"Harry's got his own problems," Quint said brusquely. "Such as Slayton."

"At least have coffee, something to eat," she implored.

"No time."

"Then let me help you," she insisted. There were more than forty animals to be led, carried or somehow wrestled up the mountain. It would be an impossible task for one man.

"No way," he shot back, and the flash in his eyes said he meant it. He was out the door before she could reply.

Miranda stared after him stubbornly. She was tired of being treated like a china doll. She was sick of being a burden. The doctor had told her to rest. She had rested. On her second visit, he had told her she seemed far better. If anything, she was more rested than Quint.

She dressed. She donned gum boots, Quint's extra slicker and an old Stetson he'd found for her that he had worn as a boy. She pulled on her leather gloves and stepped into the storm.

When Quint saw her through the downpour he merely stared at her in disgust. One of the yearling does, tranquilized, was slung over his shoulders, but he stood tall under its weight. "Get inside," he ordered. "This isn't a debutante ball."

"I'm helping," she insisted.

"You can't. Get back before I carry you in and tie you down."

She looked up at him through the water dripping off her hat brim. "You and whose army?" Her tone blazed with all her old spirit.

"You'll kill yourself," he said with even greater disgust. He started slogging up the narrow trail, the doe heavy on his wide shoulders. "You can't handle this."

"Watch me," she said with the same defiance. She made her way to the duck pen, closed the door of the baby mallards' nest box, then picked it up, groaning at its weight.

"You're supposed to be resting," he tossed back over his shoulder.

"This is an emergency," she shot back. "How could I possibly rest?" Setting her teeth, she followed Quint up the steep trail. She almost kept pace with him.

He returned, tranquilized another doe, this one larger, and hoisted it to his shoulders. Miranda put a leash on Bump's collar and led him, struggling and recalcitrant, up the mountain. When she reached the top, she decided she might as well have carried him on her back. She was exhausted.

But she managed to make her way back down the slick and treacherous mountain path once again. Quint handled the large animals, tranquilizing most of them first. He swore and grumbled how he hated to pump drugs into them. But he kept his harsh and driving pace.

Miranda did her best to keep up, ignoring his repeated orders to return to the cabin. At last, in frustration, he quit giving them. He had enough to do without fighting a crazy woman determined to kill herself with work. The trail was steep, treacherously slippery, the rain cold and, when it gusted, almost blinding.

Groggily she estimated it was midmorning when Quint struggled with the last and heaviest of the deer, a young buck with an injured leg. Miranda tagged far behind, trying to lug a caged hawk.

This time she stumbled when she reached the emergency shelters. Quint moved quickly enough to catch her. He took the hawk cage and set it under a crude wooden awning, then returned to her.

He put his hands on her arms, gripping tightly. "Miranda," he said with surprising gentleness. "You've done enough. You've helped more than I can tell. But go back now. I mean it."

She shook her head. "I'll work as long as you do," she insisted.

His grip on her arms strengthened. "No."

"Don't argue with me, Quint Wilcox," she retorted, although her voice was weak. "We've got animals down there yet."

"You're more important than they are," he said almost fiercely.

Miranda felt slightly dizzy. Perhaps it was from no food, too much exertion, too much tension. Impossibly the rain seemed to be slowing. That frightened her. It was like a hallucination.

"We've got work to do," she said again, her breathing ragged. "Just—let me rest a minute. There's still Albert and the foxes. And the eagle and big raccoons."

"I said," he repeated, "you're more important."

"No," she insisted, still dazed. The rain suddenly seemed gone. Perhaps her brain simply refused to let it register anymore.

"Yes," he said. His hands moved higher, gripping her shoulders. "Yes," he repeated, gently wiping the rain from her cheeks.

She swayed lightly, as much from his nearness as from her own fatigue. His handsome, ascetic face almost filled her vision, yet behind him she noticed something strange. A small patch of blue sky gleamed, shining like an aura around him.

"Quint?" she said weakly. "I think the rain stopped. Am I dreaming?"

He looked up, wary, disbelieving. The rain that fell on them dripped not from the sky but from the branches above.

A sudden and unexpected balminess began to suffuse the air. Somewhere a mockingbird tried an experimental carol. And behind Quint, Miranda saw a gray cloud suddenly turn silver: the sun.

"It's stopped?" she asked in exhausted disbelief.

"Yes." He tipped her hat back, stroked the damp gold bands of her bangs from her forehead.

"Has it stopped for good?" she asked, almost beseeching him. She grew more conscious of the nearness of his face, the sudden gentleness of his normally stern lips.

"Maybe. At least we've got breathing space."

She smiled up at him, almost laughing. "You mean we made it?"

He nodded, smiling back. He had such a beautiful smile, Miranda thought weakly. She wished she could see it more often, wished she could make it appear. But that seemed impossible.

At least they had worked together, she thought proudly. Worked together and hard and well. Her smile grew more tremulous. His suddenly disappeared. Something far more serious than camaraderie came into his eyes. He gave her look that burned into her heart.

Before she realized what was happening, he wrapped her in his arms, holding her so tightly she could hardly breathe. Her hat had dropped to the ground and he laid his cheek against the damp waves of her hair. He gave his rare, short, deep laugh again. "We made it."

Other patches of blue appeared in the sky. Sunlight, cool yet bright, suddenly shone in the clearing. Other birds began to join the mockingbird in heralding the return of sunshine.

"Listen to them," he said in her ear. "They know. They always do. It's really over. The worst part."

"I don't believe it," she said, exhausted yet exhilarated, clinging to him more tightly than she should.

"Trust the birds," he said, his lips hot against her ear. "The wild things know. I think we're safe, soldier."

"Soldier?" she asked half-dreamily. Her cheek pressed against the harsh, wet surface of his slicker. She could feel the strong and invincible beating of his heart beneath.

"Soldier," he repeated cryptically. "My soldier. My dependable one. My prettiest girl, and best."

She pressed her face harder against his chest. Her arms were around his neck, tightly, as if more than anything she feared he might let her go. "Quint . . ." she said helplessly.

"Miranda," he murmured. He kissed the side of her neck. His touch swept through her like leaping waves of magic. Then almost roughly, he took her chin in his hand and turned her face up to his. His darker eyes stared hypnotically into her gray-green ones, then his mouth swept down to take hers with a hunger and a passion that dizzied her again.

The ferocity of his desire made her light-headed, dazzled, a creature of warmth and tumult. His mouth moved on hers, claiming it, storming it, teaching it, teasing it. The commanding seduction of it filled her with a yearning somewhere between ecstasy and madness.

One strong hand pulled her against him so tightly she thought their bodies might actually merge. His other hand kept her face imprisoned in his strong fingers so his mouth continued its sweet and total piracy of hers. She could not have resisted him if she wanted, and she did not want to resist, now or ever. His lips, his tongue, wrested all the secrets of her own. They told her she was his; she no longer had any choice.

Then, with an almost desperate swiftness, his hands were stripping away the slickers, hers and his. Their clothing was damp beneath, and when she wound her arms around him once again, she could feel his muscles moving like live sculpture under the moistness of his shirt, feel the heat of his thighs through the wet denim.

His lips could not leave hers. His mouth would stray to the smoothness of her cheek, the feathery curve of her eyebrow, the pounding pulse in her jaw, yet always return to her eager lips as if ravenous, famished, perishing for the taste of her. He smelled of wildness and rain. His unshaven face burned against hers. He kissed her as a man dying of thirst might drink from a life-giving spring. It was as if, starving for her, he took her kisses with a completeness that bordered on frenzy.

His hands, demanding yet giving, moved to her breasts, swollen beneath the dampness of her cotton shirt. Lean fingers fumbled with her buttons, drew aside the shirt. He kissed her more ardently as he touched her breasts beneath the lacy covering of her bra.

He struggled a brief moment to unveil them completely, then drew back, giving her a tight and possessive smile. "Excuse this," he said, the muscle in his jaw moving hard. With one strong movement he undid her bra and let it fall away. The action had more hunger than finesse. She was naked to his heated, exploring touch, and his hands took possession of her bare breasts. She bloomed beneath the tender mastery of his stroking claims, her rosy nipples, pointing, firming, straining to be taken by him.

He managed once more to draw his lips from hers. With agonizing slowness he trailed kisses to her throat, her shoulder, then the tantalizing sweetness of her breasts. Miranda shuddered in yearning joy as she felt the heat of his lips, the silky ravishment of his tongue.

He dropped to his knees before her. His hands returned to worship her breasts, caress the slim sweep of her waist, then cup her breasts again. His lips pressed hotly against her midriff, kissing the satiny skin, setting her arched body ablaze.

"Quint," she moaned. She bent to press his dark head more intimately against her flesh. Legs weak, she, too, went to her knees. Breathless, she took his face between her trembling hands, kissing him full on his lips again and again. "Quint," she repeated helplessly.

Then, suddenly, he stilled and drew away. Slowly his hands moved from her waist to her bared shoulders. He inhaled deeply. He looked at her face, drugged and glowing with passion, the loveliness of her bare flesh.

He stood abruptly, pulling her to her feet. He looked down at her with eyes that were both desirous and haunted, staring at her with that dangerous expression for a long minute. Then he looked away, as if he'd suddenly changed his mind about wanting her, although she could see the pulse leaping in his bronzed neck.

He released her, picked up her shirt and drew it back on, fastening it. The slightest brush of his fingers made her burn with pleasure. But he seemed to have withdrawn into himself.

Hastily, ashamed of her response to him, she took up her slicker, put it on. She picked up her lacy bra furtively, hiding it in her pocket. Without looking at him, she reached for her hat.

His own slicker had already been thrown about his shoulders like a cape. He had pulled back into himself with startling completeness. He stared at the forest for a moment, then his eyes met hers. "Sorry," he said, his face cold and without emotion.

"Are you?" she asked, wounded, for she wasn't sorry at all.

He nodded. "Yes. Sorry. All your life men have wanted you, Miranda."

So that's it, she thought with weariness that seemed as chill as death. *He still thinks that's all I am. The flibberti-gibbet. The flirt. The girl for cheap thrills.* She drew the slicker more tightly about herself. She felt suddenly exhausted, almost sick.

His hat was pushed back on the damp waves of his dark hair. He studied her with the utmost seriousness. "A lot of men have wanted you," he repeated. He reached out his forefinger, tipped her chin up so she had to look him full in the face. "And I'm no better. But only at the right time. And in the right way. Not like this. And not now."

"I don't know what you mean," she breathed.

"I'm not sure I do myself," he said, unsmiling.

To her surprise, he took her hand and began leading her down the perilous, still-slippery mountain path. She followed in confusion. For a moment they had both surrendered to that mutual desire, strong and surging as the wild river that had been rising so inexorably.

"What are we going to do now?" she asked timorously. It was a vague question. She was afraid to ask a specific one.

"We take showers," he said with his rare sideways grin "Separately. If cold water can't slow me down, I won' chance hot. Then food. Then you take a nap while I arrange the rest of these animals."

"Will we have to move them all back down?" she asked, hoping he would say no.

"Not yet." He shook his head. "They're more work to feed and tend, but if the rain starts again, they're safe."

They walked in silence back to the cabin. The sun shone down brightly, as if it had never been absent. When they reached the door of the cabin, she couldn't leave him, couldn't move inside. Mesmerized, she stared up into his face, which wore that puzzling expression of intense desire and even more intense control. "If—if the rain stops—really stops," she said at last, "will you still send me away?"

Such a bald question, she thought, and filled with such transparent yearning.

He shook his head enigmatically. "I don't know. You're not safe here any longer. You're not safe from me."

Then he turned and headed toward the eagle cage. She wasn't sure what he meant when he said he wanted her—but at the right time and in the right way. She only knew she was his already. And knowing that, she was inexplicably and completely happy for the first time in her life.

CHAPTER NINE

THE FIRST DAY of what Quint called Operation Ark passed in exhaustion. Miranda napped easily for once, without even wanting to. She awoke at dusk, made a simple supper and saw how toilworn Quint looked.

Trusting neither the sun nor the revised weather reports, he'd kept working while Miranda slept. When he was sure the animals in both sets of shelters were safe and their dwellings secure, he started clearing trees to make a proper road to the higher shelter. He'd spent the late afternoon and even the twilight hours with a chain saw, felling cedars. Yet as he leaned against the back of his chair, he looked restless, as if he were ready to go saw down trees in the moonlight.

"I think," she said carefully, "I should call your father and tell him we have to postpone the party."

His coffee cup stopped halfway to his lips. He straightened in his chair. "No," he said curtly. "You've worked too hard."

"And you've worked too hard here," Miranda said firmly. "If I know you, you'll keep on working. You can't seem to stop."

He shrugged moodily. "Momentum," he grumbled. "A break'd be good. I can call somebody to cover me a couple days. If the weather holds, we'll go to Cherry Creek. You want to, don't you?"

"What I want isn't important," Miranda protested. After the trauma of the past few days, the party, which she had once anticipated so eagerly, seemed of no consequence.

He gave her an unreadable glance and took another sip of coffee. "It's important to Duke. Do it for him," he said at last, setting down his cup and pushing it away. He stretched, yawned, then rose.

"Where are you going?" Miranda asked in alarm.

"Out. I want to check the animals once more. And I've been thinking about the house. I want to check possible sites, too. When I build a house, it might be best to put the whole shebang, shelters and all, up on the mountain. The river may rise this high only once every two hundred years, but that's too often."

"Quint—" she began to protest.

He bent and laid his forefinger against the softness of her lips. "Hush," he said. "Be good and I'll show you the house plans tomorrow night. Before the party."

"But—"

"Hush," he repeated. His finger caressed the curves of her upper lip, his thumb rested on the warmth of her lower one.

For once in her life, Miranda hushed.

"I'M TERRIFIED!" Miranda cried in a mock-tragic voice. She was having a large, economy-sized attack of predinner party jitters.

"You'll do fine," Quint consoled her. "Are you sure this tie is right? Is it supposed to cut off my air supply?"

She turned to Quint, who looked both handsome and uncomfortable in his tux. They were in Duke's study, a large room with floor-to-ceiling windows overlooking the dusky blue of Cherrytree Lake. The house, the closest thing Miranda had ever seen to a true Southern mansion, was exqui-

site, if anything so gigantic could also be called exquisite.
Mechanically she reached up to straighten his tie.

"It looks perfect," she replied, readjusting it anyway.
"Of course it's supposed to cut off your air. How would you
know you were dressed up if you weren't uncomfortable?"

"Are you uncomfortable?" he teased. She looked rav-
ishing. Her thick blond hair was heaped with artful care-
lessness atop her head, spilling shining curls around her
small ears and the nape of her graceful neck. Her dress, of
muted yet rich purple, was long, clinging and simple. Floor-
length, sleeveless, it was high in front, discreetly low in
back. She wore little makeup, and her only jewelry was a
pair of amethyst earrings.

"Women are used to being uncomfortable," she said with
more cheer than she felt. "Do I look all right? Not too—you
know—too overdone?"

He resisted the urge to put his hands on her golden
shoulders and stroke the velvety skin of her arms. "You
look fine," he muttered gruffly. He turned from her, sensing how hard she had struggled to do things right. "Come
on," he rasped, moving across the room. "I'll show you the
house I'm going to build on the Flirtation."

Quint walked over to the large architect's drafting board
by the window and Miranda followed. Sketches and a set of
floor plans rested on its tilted surface, and she peered
around from behind him to have a look.

"Oh," she said with an involuntary gasp. "It's beautiful!"

The long and sweeping lines of the wood-and-brick frame
were modern yet surprisingly graceful. A sunken living room
with fireplace and floor-to-ceiling bookcases, an enormous
kitchen and an even more enormous master bedroom with
sliding-glass doors to a flagstone patio were among the features.

"Do you really like it?" he asked. He stepped away from her slightly, because her perfume made him want to kiss her behind the ears. Since their encounter a few days before he'd found himself full of dangerous impulses. "I worked a long time on it. I wanted it comfortable—but not ostentatious. Ostentation wouldn't fit in with the foundation."

"You designed it all?" she asked. "It's perfect. It'll fit in with the mountains and the river as naturally as the trees."

She paused, suddenly uncomfortable. "You're sure," she asked hesitantly, "*I* don't look too ostentatious? I want to look right for the board, and the foundation."

He turned, fiddled with his hated tie and glanced down at her. She looked like a princess to him, a beautiful and vulnerable princess. "You look fine," he repeated, his voice noncommittal. Then, because she still had that inexplicably fragile air about her, he added, "You're perfect yourself."

She smiled up at him with something akin to shyness. Nobody had ever before called her perfect.

"Do you really think the party will be all right?" she asked.

He gave her his slanted one-eighth of a smile. "Do all women get like this before a party?"

"I think so," she admitted ruefully.

"Relax," he said, putting his hands in his pockets so he'd stop being tempted to reach out and touch the gold of her spilling curls. "It'll be perfect, too."

Quint was right. The party was perfect. Miranda called on resources she didn't know she had. For years she had watched Jaqueline engineer such events with expert calculation. She made use of her observations of that shrewd expertise and added to it her own instincts of warmth and fun. She was equally careful to downplay the flamboyance behind which she had hidden for years.

She delighted to find herself performing minor miracles that night. Somehow she kept Mrs. Petitjean relatively calm.

Against all odds, Miranda had arranged everything just right, even though she had never seen the house before that weekend. Most important, she made the guests feel comfortable. Mrs. Lucius Burnside, a perpetually unsmiling woman, smiled repeatedly. Mr. Robert Jefferson Davis, a painfully shy man, felt so at home that he relaxed and even told a joke. She somehow made Mr. Lionel Figg, who tended to talk too much, sink periodically into a happy and polite silence. Most difficult of all, she felt that she made Quint nearly comfortable with his hated duties as host and that perhaps he had even enjoyed the evening a bit.

She drew him out carefully at dinner, making him tell the guests of the foundation's work, its link with the Wilderness Conservancy, his own labors on the Flirtation, even anecdotes about the animals, especially Ratso, Bump and the difficult Albert, who was finally rallying.

After dessert, Mrs. Lucius Burnside buttonholed Miranda while the men enjoyed brandy and cigars.

Gnarled fingers curled tightly around Miranda's arm, Mrs. Burnside steered her to the privacy of Duke's columned porch. She tapped Miranda on the shoulder with her fan. "I don't know what you've done to that young man," Mrs. Burnside said in her tart voice. "Quinton has always been such a silent, difficult person. You've brought out a side of him I hadn't seen. You are a formidable young woman."

"Why—thank you—I think," Miranda laughed, taken aback by the woman's bluntness.

Mrs. Burnside's wizened face, looking like that of an elderly elf, wrinkled even more as she stared up to study Miranda.

"You're a young woman of uncertain reputation," she asserted. "At least so I have read."

This time Miranda cringed. She could think of no reply. She had spent the whole evening trying to defy that reputation.

"Think nothing of it," Mrs. Burnside commanded. She lightly rapped Miranda again with her folded ivory fan. "I myself have a reputation as an eccentric. Also as a woman without humor. I am not eccentric, merely more sensible than most. I am not humorless, but neither do I find life a laughing matter. As for reputations, I judge people for myself, not by what others say. Anyone who does otherwise is a fool and a popinjay. Deny it if you wish. It is true."

Miranda, still taken aback, had no response. Embarrassed, she stood in silence, staring down into the brightly glinting eyes of Mrs. Burnside.

"I can read," the woman said acerbically. "Your life has had its less than promising episodes. So did mine. So did Quinton's. He survived them. Yet all such episodes change us. Not always for the better. I sense in you the spirit of a survivor. The strength to turn ill to good. It is the most valuable of all gifts. Use it."

The strange little woman, staring up at her so fixedly in the moonlight, made Miranda almost giddy. She felt as if she were having an encounter with some sort of outspoken fairy godmother.

"Quint," Miranda managed to say, "had unhappy episodes?" Always she had sensed a dark side to him, some hidden truth that separated him from other men.

Mrs. Burnside turned and looked at the azalea bushes silvered by the moonlight. "I am not a gossip," she said crustily. "But you'll hear the story eventually, so you may as well hear the truth." She straightened the chiffon scarf around her wrinkled throat.

"You see," she said, still gazing at the azaleas, "there was an accident. Quinton was sixteen. He was driving—speeding, as wild boys are wont to do. Three of them were in the car. They'd had a drink or two—as wild boys are also wont to do. Two beers apiece, I believe. Another driver ran a stop sign on a country road. Quinton swerved, lost control of the car. His best friend, Edward Dumas, was killed. His younger brother, Jerry, was badly hurt—a concussion, broken ribs, two cracked vertebrae. They wondered for a time if Jerry would ever use his legs again. But Quinton walked away from that crushed car without a scratch."

"No." Miranda breathed. She put her hands to her breast. She could feel the horrified thudding of her heart.

"Yes." Mrs. Burnside turned and cast a glittering look at Miranda. "His best friend was dead. His brother came close to death, and he himself was untouched. It was a terrible burden of guilt for a boy so young to bear. He was ultimately cleared of serious wrongdoing. The other driver was more at fault."

"But that wouldn't matter to Quint," Miranda almost whispered.

"You're astute," Mrs. Burnside said briskly. "The guilt nearly destroyed him. The community was unkind. Many said Quinton was absolved only because of Duke's wealth and influence. The boy drove himself to every sort of excess—every kind of wildness. It was as if he wanted to join Edward Dumas in the grave—believed he deserved to."

"How did he ever go on?" Miranda asked, her throat tight. She knew how powerful and how deep Quint's emotions ran. The thought of him in such anguish pained her profoundly.

"Ah." Mrs. Burnside opened her ivory fan with a flourish, then snapped it shut again. "His parents. Duke and Frances. Ultimately Jerry, too. I have never seen a family stand behind a troubled member with the steadfastness that they did. It was as if through that love, they willed him to survive and recover."

"And he did," Miranda said, turning away so Mrs. Burnside's sharp gaze wouldn't see the tears glinting in her eyes. No wonder she had become so fond of Duke. He was a supremely good man. And no wonder Quint was so appalled at the way Miranda's family responded to her troubles. They must seem like monsters to him, compared to his own parents and brother.

"He recovered for the most part," Mrs. Burnside said. She put her folded fan under Miranda's chin, forcing Miranda to turn her face back and look down at the older woman's strange, elvish face. "He became a good man, a strong man but a loner. He has found it hard to reach out to people. I have often wondered if he is capable of opening himself up enough to love. I think I should tell you this for your own sake. He may be a man incapable of loving anyone outside his family."

"What do you mean, for my sake?" Miranda asked, puzzled and troubled at the same time.

"Because you love him, of course," Mrs. Burnside pronounced. Again she toyed with her fan, but her bright little eyes did not leave Miranda's.

Miranda swallowed hard. Somewhere a whippoorwill sang and a mockingbird answered. "Does it really show that much?" she asked unhappily. She had thought herself expert at disguising her emotions.

"Oh, my dear," Mrs. Burnside replied, shaking her head in pity. "It shines out of your face like a light."

MIRANDA MOVED through the rest of the evening in a darkly thoughtful haze. Mrs. Burnside's revelations had shaken her. Yet, used to burying her feelings deeply, she kept up her cheery facade and performed the most difficult of a hostess's duties with apparent ease.

She tried to be more careful, though, about the way she looked at Quint. She wondered if love actually did shine out of her face like a light. Could everyone tell? Or only someone as eerily perceptive as Mrs. Burnside?

It was well after midnight when the last guest left. "Oh!" cried Mrs. Petitjean. "Oh, my stars and garters!" She headed straight to the kitchen to collapse with a glass of sherry.

Quint already had his tie loosened, his tuxedo jacket off, and was rolling up his sleeves. Miranda sighed, half in nervousness, half in satisfaction.

"Here," he said, refilling his glass with brandy and hers with Perrier. "This calls for a drink on the veranda."

They took their glasses and stepped out on the long porch. The scent of flowers wafted on the night air, the moonlight was bright. The whippoorwill and the mockingbird continued their melodious dialogue. Quint touched his glass to hers.

"Congratulations," he murmured. "It was perfect. You were perfect. I almost enjoyed myself."

Miranda smiled at him, her heart beating hard.

"Something must be wrong with my hearing. Did you say you almost enjoyed it?"

He sipped his brandy. "They can be a cantankerous and stuffy bunch. You must have worked a charm on them. Especially Mrs. Burnside, the old gorgon. What did she whisper in your ear when she dragged you off? I couldn't believe it when I saw the two of you out here."

He gave her his fraction of a smile. "She was talking about you," Miranda said, too disquieted by his nearness to put it less bluntly.

His smile faded. He set his glass on the railing. "Oh" was all he said.

"She told me what happened to you. When you were sixteen," she admitted. She knew he was a private man, yet she respected him too much to hide the truth.

He swore softly. "That crazy old harpy," he said, lip curling in dislike. "She can sit, staring all night without saying anything, then come out with a piece of ancient garbage like that."

Miranda could feel his anger. Its vibrations rode dark and jolting upon the air.

"I don't think she did it to be vicious," she said carefully. "I think she wanted me to understand you."

He leaned by the railing, his hands folded tightly in front of him. "What business is it of hers," he demanded coldly, "if you understand me?"

Miranda took a deep breath. For the first time in years she felt like an awkward preteen again—suddenly too tall, too shy, too uncertain.

"She thinks I'm attracted to you. And that you might hurt me. Because past complexities have made you—so solitary."

He turned swiftly, leaning his elbows on the railing, but even in that easy posture he radiated a dangerous tension. "She thinks you're attracted to me," he flung out with sarcasm. "And what do you think, Miranda? Are you? Or am I just another conquest you'd like to make in an ongoing series?"

Miranda, who had dodged half a thousand declarations of love from men she didn't like, suddenly found herself without words. Again she felt awkward and vulnerable. But she couldn't lie to him. Not even for the sake of pride, which no longer seemed important. "I'm attracted to you," she said at last. She held her chin very high. "What of it? It's my problem, isn't it?"

"Is it?" he mocked. Straightening to his full height, he walked slowly to her. The moonlight gleamed on his white shirtfront, making the shadows beneath his cheekbones more pronounced. "And Mrs. Burnside thinks I'd hurt you. What do you think?"

He placed one hand on her bare shoulder, sending a fever of frightened longing through her. His other hand lifted her chin so she had to look into his eyes. His thumb was firm against her jaw, his forefinger pressed softly, sensuously, against her lips, stroking them gently with a maddening allure.

Her breath caught in her throat. "Hurt me?" Her mind whirled with possible answers. *No. Nobody can hurt me anymore.*

But that was a lie. She thought of saying, *Yes, you could hurt me. But it wouldn't matter. I'd have something to remember you by, even if it was pain.*

But that answer was not right, either. He was not a man who would willingly cause someone pain. And if he knew how much she loved him, he would send her away to save her from herself.

So she said nothing at all.

"Silence, Miranda?" he teased, his voice low. "That's not your usual style. Would I hurt you? Never." His face bent closer to hers. "I think I've finally come to understand you. And the last thing I want is to hurt you. That's why I'm going to leave you here."

Miranda stiffened beneath his touch. His finger, stroking her lips, seemed suddenly like a warning to be silent and obedient. "Leave me?" she cried with real hurt in her voice

Both his hands framed her face now. "I made promises about you, Miranda. I'm not sure I can keep them. I don't want to take you back to the Flirtation."

"But why?" she begged. She put her hands on his shoulders in the age-old gesture of beseechment. He glanced at them as if her touch troubled him, but he did nothing except continue to frame her face and stare down at her, his expression unreadable in the shadows.

"Because you'll be safe here. And more comfortable. And I think if I get security guards, I can settle Mrs. Petitjean down enough to accept the idea. And Pop will be home in two weeks."

"I don't want to be here," she protested desperately. "I want to be with you. At the river. I won't bother you—I promise."

Then his hands tensed on either side of her face. "Bother me? You've bothered me from the moment I set eyes on you—you bother me till I'm half-insane with wanting you."

"If you want me, then have me," Miranda said recklessly. "Because I want you, too."

"Don't talk like that," he ordered roughly. But his arms went around her with an ardor that was almost cruel. His kiss, bruising in its intensity, made her senses whirl and surge, drinking in her mind, her will, her very soul. He pressed his fingers against her silk-covered ribs, then the pressure of his hands grew gentler, yet tense, as they explored the smooth curves of the length of her body. When his touch found the bare flesh of her back, she felt his questing mouth gasp against her own.

The softness of her straining breasts was crushed beneath the unyielding hardness of his chest, and when her gently exploring tongue met the more authoritative and adventurous claims of his own, she felt him gasp again. His hands ran obsessively, possessively, over her bare back.

Her arms wound around his neck, answering his primitive need with her own. She ran her fingers through the dark thickness of his hair, over the harsh planes of his face, the sinews of his neck.

Incandescent heat filled her blood, and the power of his ardor made it flame more whitely, blinding her to everything but his touch.

His mouth enkindled hers with its animal hunger and frightening expertise. His torridness shook the breath from her body. Then, maddeningly gentle, his kisses teased, nibbling, nuzzling, his tongue caressing, barely touching, then thrusting, demanding, challenging.

Suddenly he swept her up into his arms. Miranda was vaguely conscious that she had lost one of her purple slippers and that her carefully coiffed hair was coming down. Her breath came in something like sobs, and she felt almost helpless as she lay her heated face against his ruffled shirtfront.

She felt Quint carrying her down the wide stairs of the veranda, through the azalea gardens, yet she was too weak to protest or to question where he bore her. She kept one arm wound tightly around his neck, as if she feared losing the potent intoxication of his touch. The other hand was curled around the edge of his opened collar, loving the starched feel of the cloth, his skin, the brush against her fingers of the dark hair at the base of his throat.

He set her down with a swift and sweeping movement that made her long skirt flutter in the moonlight, yet still he held her so tightly that she was supported by his arms. Her toes barely touched the ground. It was his strength that held her upright.

Her head fell back in acquiescence to whatever he wanted of her. Her long golden hair spilled in luxuriant disorder down her back.

"This is the folly, Miranda," he almost hissed against her lips. "And perhaps nights like this are why it's named a folly. Do you understand what I'm saying?"

Half-faint, she managed to look at the scene before her. Newly blooming roses surrounded the garden paths, the richness of their perfume overwhelming. They stood beside a stone structure of such oddness it might have come from a fairy tale. It was hidden from the main house by a thick grove of tulip trees.

Vaguely Miranda recognized the bizarre edifice was precisely what Quint had called it—a folly. Such eccentric buildings had been the rage among the European rich in earlier centuries. She had seen many in France; they often resembled small, semiruined castles. Other than supplying a moody ornamental touch, they served no purpose and were aptly named "follies." Duke, in a moment of extravagance or humor, must have commissioned this one, complete with arched doors and a small turreted tower.

"I said," Quint repeated, his fingers digging into her arms even more passionately, "this is a folly. Do you know what that means?"

"A—building. Fanciful building," she said, wishing his touch were gentler.

"There's still a bed in there," he said, his voice taking on a harshness she wasn't sure she understood. "I used to hide out here in the old days when I didn't want to face anything—including myself."

"A bed?" she asked, fear suddenly mingling with her desire.

"You know what else a folly is?" he demanded, giving her a slight but vigorous shake. "It's foolishness. The kind that ends in disaster. And we're on its threshold. Do you really want to walk into it? Do you?"

She shook her head in pained confusion. "You're hurting me," she said, trying to hold back the tears.

"And you're hurting me," he replied with vehemence. "Haven't you learned anything, Miranda? I said I wanted you. I don't want to want you, but I do. When you tell me you want me, I come close to losing control. And you don't understand."

"Understand what?" she implored him, trying to shake free from his iron embrace.

But he held her tighter still, until she had to struggle to keep from whimpering. "That wanting and loving are two different things. You don't understand—or remember that we both promised this madness wouldn't happen. And it is madness. Just because I want you doesn't mean I love you. Or that you love me."

She went nearly limp in his arms. "You don't know anything about me," she said with bitterness.

"I know more about you than you know yourself," he replied. His grip on her arms loosened slightly, became less cruel. "You're young. Confused. I promised to take care of you. Instead, I'm about to take you into the darkness of folly—very real folly. Do you really want to go?"

She almost sagged but managed to hold herself erect. With an unexpected surge of energy, she brushed his hands away. He had told her he didn't love her, he merely wanted her, and that meant he was no different than hundreds of men she had known. No, there was one difference. To her sorrow, she loved him.

She held her chin high, she stroked her hair back into a semblance of order. "I want nothing from you," she said haughtily. Miranda, wounded, could sound extraordinarily haughty.

"Nothing?" he taunted. "I'm not so sure. I think what you want is simple. But our situation's complex."

She sighed with weariness. She removed her remaining sandal. "I'd like some simple things, all right," she said frostily. "Consideration. Consistency. Perhaps even an ordinary 'thank you' once in a while. And perhaps—just perhaps—as much kindness from time to time as you show a common animal."

She turned her back on him and walked toward the house. She knew where her guest room was and how to find her way. She just hoped she could make it past the watchful eyes of Mrs. Petitjean.

"Miranda!" Quint shouted after her, but she did not turn. She kept walking. Her long blond hair swung and gleamed in the moonlight.

"Miranda!" he cried again. "I can't take you back with me tomorrow. Can't you see that?"

She did not bother to answer. She had tried as hard as she could to make someone love her. As usual, she had failed. But it didn't affect her bearing in the slightest. She walked away like a queen. She was an excellent loser. She always had been.

CHAPTER TEN

As it happened, Miranda returned to the Flirtation with Quint after all. First, Mrs. Petitjean, frazzled almost to the point of breakdown now that the party was over, reached new depths of excitability.

"She's a lovely girl, but I can't have her here!" the woman whined, sitting at the kitchen table.

"I'll hire a guard," Quint said between his teeth. Miranda was keeping to her room, for which he was profoundly grateful.

"You don't understand," Mrs. Petitjean accused tearfully. "First your father nearly gets killed—then I have to get this party together completely by telephone—you don't understand what a strain a big party is—"

"I'm beginning to understand why I hate them," Quint muttered.

"And now you want me to stay here alone with this girl who's being pursued by a maniac," Mrs. Petitjean practically wailed. She blew her nose unceremoniously into a paper towel. "She's an absolutely wonderful girl, but I swear I heard prowlers all night long, creeping around the house, looking for a way in to murder us all."

"I seriously doubt Miranda is actually menaced," Quint replied impatiently. "I can practically guarantee she isn't—"

"Famous last words!" moaned Mrs. Petitjean. "I'm a sensitive person. Very nervous. I've been under great strain.

I'd hate to call your father and tell him I'm quitting right now, but—well, Quinton, you have no right to torture me this way.''

Women, he thought with disgust. He strode angrily from the kitchen into his father's study, picked up the phone and dialed the hospital.

"How'd the party go?" his father demanded without preliminary.

"Fine," Quint practically snapped. "But about this girl. I can't—"

"Did a bang-up job, did she? Grew up around this sort of thing, she did. People probably had fun for once. Probably best one we've ever had, right?"

"It probably was," Quint agreed without enthusiasm. "But I can't take her back to the Flirtation with me. Things are getting too complicated. And Mrs. Petitjean won't let her stay here. She gets hysterical if I mention it."

"Emma Petitjean was born hysterical," Duke answered gruffly. "She's spent her life being hysterical. But the woman can cook. And clean like a demon. And what in hell about the girl is getting too complicated?"

Quint paused, groping for the right words. "Pop, my taking her was not such a good idea. I'm not a monk. She's a fairly attractive woman."

"Fairly!" roared Duke. "What's this *fairly* business? She's a knockout. Don't tell me you finally noticed? I mean, you live like a monk."

"Of course I noticed," Quint shot back. "And it's difficult having a perfectly healthy man and woman cooped up together. It's not—right."

"It's not right only if things get out of hand," Duke practically shouted. "I gave my word the poor girl would be taken care of—now all of a sudden you're like some teenage kid who can't control himself. You? After you gave your word? Which up to now has been practically sacred? I don't believe it for a minute. She's not your type. She's too lively, too gregarious for you. Not that you don't need that. Just put up with her a while longer. And keep your hands off her. I'll be home in two weeks. Then I'll handle things. Arrgh! The younger generation."

"Even if you take her, Mrs. Petitjean won't put up with it," Quint insisted. "We've got to find another place for the girl—now."

"I'll handle Mrs. Petitjean," Duke practically bellowed. "You just don't know how, Quinton. In the meantime, the girl's got a place to stay—the Flirtation. When this family makes a promise it keeps it, by doggies. Now are you and Miranda going to stop on the way back and see me or not?"

"I suppose," Quint said fatalistically.

"Good," said Duke. "Bring me a pound of peanut brittle, a bag of those little bitty colored marshmallows and a book with lots of spies and shooting in it."

Quint agreed, his jaw set like granite. He marched up the stairs and beat on Miranda's door. He muttered her name.

"Go away," she said without opening the door. "I'm not hungry. I'd starve to death before I'd eat in the same house with you."

"Then prepare to starve," he snarled back. "Because you're coming back to the river with me. Pack. We're leaving in half an hour."

Thirty seconds of silence passed. The door opened just enough for Miranda to peer out at him with hurt suspicion. She still had on her purple dress, he noticed unhappily. She'd probably come in, thrown herself on the bed and cried herself to sleep—after all the work she'd done on the party. He felt lower than a cotton rat and as if he'd been more evil-tempered than that cursed alligator.

"What makes you think I'd go back with you?" she asked, her lower lip jutting out like a stubborn child's.

"Because," he said with more coldness than he felt, "neither of us has much choice."

She eyed him with disbelief. "You mean you changed your mind?" she asked, her face revealing nothing.

"Yes," he said with an equal lack of emotion. "I changed my mind. I said I'd take care of you, and I will. I can handle you. And six like you."

She stared up at him, her gray-green eyes defiant beneath their long lashes. "Think so, eh?"

"You bet," he answered silkily.

"Optimist," Miranda returned just as silkily and with just as much challenge.

"Pack," he said.

THREE AND A HALF hours later, after a side trip to the hospital to see Duke, the van stopped at the entry road to the property. Quint got out, gathered the mail, stuck the bundle under the visor and drove silently down the lane to the cabin. He had been less communicative than usual. He was probably in a grudging mood because in addition to everything else, Duke had insisted the new house on the Flirtation be started immediately. And he and Quint had agreed, unhappily, that the complex of animal shelters should be moved higher permanently.

Quint unloaded the van while Miranda, delighted to see Bump again, whirled and played with him. Quint paid Jamie McIver, who had stayed with the animals, and questioned him about how things had gone. The river had sunk to near-normal level and the sun shone brightly, as if the rains had never been.

After Jamie left, the two of them settled wordlessly into the cabin. When Miranda came out of the bedroom, clad in her safari shorts and matching shirt, Quint was sitting at the table, his face taut.

"Good news, bad news," he said, his cobalt eyes measuring her dispassionately. "Sit down."

She sat, crossing her legs and tossing her hair back. She heard Ratso outside the window rasping, "Welcome home, welcome home, what's to eat?"

"What's the good news?" she asked, trying to give him a look as steady as his own.

He tossed two business-size envelopes on the table before her. "You just made the Wilderness Conservancy about three hundred thousand dollars. You write a good fundraising letter. Two separate donors."

Miranda's artificial cool evaporated. "Really?" she asked happily. "Donations?" She opened the envelopes excitedly and gazed with pleasure at the two checks. She smiled broadly at Quint. "All right!" she said with her old natural enthusiasm. "That'll buy you a little more wilderness, eh?"

But he wasn't smiling. She put the checks on the table. Her own smile faded. "What's the bad news?" she asked, suddenly apprehensive.

He was silent a moment, his mouth grim. He handed her another envelope, also business size. Miranda flinched uncontrollably. The envelope had a horrible familiarity about it.

"I'm sorry," he said bluntly. "Your friend's caught up with you."

"Oh, no," she wanted to say. But she was incapable of speech. With trembling hands she opened the letter. It was a single typewritten sheet of paper whose appearance she knew all too well.

As she unfolded it, Quint got up and stood behind her. For all her confusion and resentment concerning him, she was suddenly achingly glad he was there. She knew he was reading over her shoulder, looking at the terrible words as if he could take their burden on himself. She wished he would touch her, in comfort, but she knew he would not.

Dear hussy glamor girl easy thing
It took me sum time but I found you at last and now your bolder than ever, arent you, living with your LATEST paramour? Do you have no shame at all?? You reelly are a bad, loose, no good. But you cant hide frum me. I am close, Miranda. I get closer too you all the time. I know evry move you make. I can find you anywear in this country. I followed you hear, I will follow you home. Better hide again.

The Watcher

PS You may think your new boyfriend is pretty hot stuff but he cant proteck you frum me if I decide to come for you.

Miranda crumpled the note and swore brokenly. With a moan she collapsed, burying her face in her arms. She tried to keep from sobbing.

She felt Quint behind her, wished fervently he would bend down, draw her to him, hold her. Instead, he pried the crushed letter from her tense fingers. "Let me see it," he ordered. She had no strength to resist him.

"Is he really here?" she asked, her voice hardly more than a whisper. "Is he really watching?"

"No," he said curtly. "The postmark's Alexandria again. Whoever it is is trying to scare you. Don't let them."

Miranda made a sound halfway between a laugh and a sob.

"Miranda!" he said sharply. "Get hold of yourself. I asked you once if I could see the other letters. I think it's time. Get them."

Numbly she rose, went to her bedroom and returned with the letters. She had them bound together with a wisp of black ribbon, as if they were a set of perverse love letters.

She handed him the bundle. "You were right last night," she said dully. "I shouldn't have come back here. I might be putting you in danger. He says you can't protect me."

Quint sat in the chair she had vacated. He unbound the letters and spread them out before him. "Then he doesn't know me, does he?" he asked. "I said I'd take care of you. I can and I will. Nobody's going to hurt you, Miranda. Physically at least."

How could he be so calm? she wondered, wanting to scream at him, at her unseen tormentor, at the world itself. "Sit down," he commanded. "I need to ask you some questions."

"It won't do any good."

"Sit," he ordered again. In his quiet way he was as implacable as Duke. Apathetically she obeyed. He grilled her mercilessly.

He asked every sort of question, about her last year in school, whom she had dated, whom she hadn't dated, whom she might have met in Washington or Georgetown on vacation. He sometimes asked things that seemed totally irrelevant. Miranda grew more upset and impatient. She had been through the whole fruitless inquiry in her own mind a thousand times.

"Okay," he persisted, "try again. What happened right before you got the first letter? Think hard. Did you meet anybody new? Could you have made anybody mad?"

"I told you," she said wearily, putting her head in her hands. "Nothing happened. I went home for Thanksgiving. I went out with a young congressman with buckteeth and roaming fingers. I didn't like him, but I wasn't rude to him. He wasn't really interested in me anyway—not as a person. Just as a body.''

She heard the bitterness in her last statement and hated it.

"How can you be sure?"

"He was one of Jaqueline's castoffs," Miranda explained, struggling to stay patient. "He was interested in a woman who'd fit into the Washington power structure—and that is most definitely not me. Jaqueline was just getting involved with Delbert then, I think. She encouraged me to go out with the other one—Fred. That's his name."

"Why did she encourage you to go out with him?"

"She said he'd always been attracted to me." Miranda shrugged. "She'd gone with him a bit during the summer when I was home. But she said he was shallow." She laughed. "Which, of course, was probably why he was attracted to me. At any rate, Jaqueline didn't find him up to snuff."

"Did this happen often?" Quint asked, cocking an eyebrow.

"That she passed one of her beaux on to me?" Miranda asked. "A few times. It was useless, really. We never liked the same type. But for some reason she'd decide a certain man was really for me, not her. I don't know why. I'd try to be friendly to them, but they were never my type."

"But she didn't with this Delbert?" Quint probed.

"Oh, Delbert was different from the start for Jaqueline," Miranda explained tiredly. "She said he was just like Daddy—only even brighter, more ambitious and more affectionate. Daddy isn't affectionate. And Delbert had eyes only for Jaqueline once they met. That's important to her."

"You never met him?" Quint asked carefully.

"Something always came up," Miranda said. Her head was starting to hurt. Hadn't she explained this all before? "He even sent me a note once, right before Christmas, saying he hoped we'd get to meet. But we didn't."

"What happened?"

"At Christmas, Jaqueline came down with some sort of terrible flu. She begged me not to come home. I mean, I could get sick and go back to school and spread it."

"You didn't go home at Christmas?" he asked, cocking his eyebrow again.

"I stayed in the dorm," Miranda said, making a face. "A few of the exchange students stayed, too. I got chased around the Christmas tree in the lobby by the student from Kharakastan. I had Christmas dinner with two Nigerians and a girl from Brazil who was so homesick she cried through the whole meal."

"Did he catch you?" Quint asked, giving her his hint of a smile for the first time that day. "The student from Kharakastan?"

"Of course not," she said indignantly. "What do you think of me?"

"I don't know," he said, his smile fading. "I never have. That's part of the problem." Then he began to question her again with the same unrelenting thoroughness.

"Why do you think this person wants you out of the country?" he asked repeatedly. "Why does he want you not just away, but far away?"

"I don't know" was all she could say. She had to repeat it until it became like a meaningless chant.

At last, her patience hopelessly frayed, she said, "I can't sit here going over this any longer. I just can't. I've got to get out. Do you think I could take a walk?"

He looked at her. Her face, pale and strained, made him want to break the letter writer's neck. She looked so unlik herself—as if somebody were slowly, systematically beating her into the ground.

"You aren't in danger here," he muttered curtly. "I don't believe for a minute this person's around. You're being hounded by a coward, Miranda. And anybody fool enough to sneak onto my property takes a chance of being carried off feet first."

"How can you be so sure?" she asked, nervously twisting a strand of golden hair.

"Don't worry," he stated. "I'm sure. Nobody here will hurt you."

She stood. There was something fatalistic in her posture that it hurt him to see. "Present company excepted, of course," she said. She didn't smile.

"Present company excepted," he replied grimly. "Just be careful. Take the dog."

She straightened, smoothed her luxuriant hair back and headed for the door, obviously afire with more than her usual restlessness. He watched her go out the screen door, heard her greet Boots, then talk in a stream of affectionate nonsense to Bump.

He stood, went to the window. He watched her set off down a path, the dog running ahead of her, the crazy deer at her side, pressed close as a lover. Again he thought of how alike they were—the girl and the orphaned deer. Both half tame, half wild, beautiful and apart from their fellow creatures—foundlings.

He returned to the table and sat again. He studied the letters one more time. He was certain his theory was right. From the day it first burst into his mind like a malignant light, he was certain. He had hoped the whole matter would resolve itself. It wasn't going to. Somebody was going to have to do something. He was that somebody.

He swept the letters together and retied them. He swore. The girl had more trouble clinging to her than she could begin to understand.

But he was sure that as long as he kept her here, on the Flirtation, she was safe. He was certain. Duke was right. This was where she belonged.

MIRANDA WALKED, brooding, a long way. Her ulcer pained her, but she wouldn't tell Quint. She couldn't bear to be confined to bed again. Restlessness surged through her body until she felt almost electrified by it.

Boots, the collie, went with her halfway down the river path, but as usual, his loyalty to Quint and the wild stock called him home. He turned and trotted back the way they had come, his plumy tail waving. Bump, foolish, faithful Bump, stayed by her side. She kept her arm wound around his sleek neck.

Her thoughts were too confused to sort. She wanted to keep walking until she could walk no more. The woods lining the river grew wilder, denser. The path narrowed until Bump could no longer walk by her side. He followed behind, keeping as close as he could, butting her from time to time with his black nose.

Quint had brought her back. Brought her home. No, she thought unhappily, this wasn't her home. And he didn't really want her there. She guessed, from the conversation they'd had with Duke in the hospital earlier, that it was Duke's decree that changed Quint's mind. Why Duke was so protective of her, so kind to her, was simply another mystery.

The letters were like a nightmare turning into full-time reality. Who could resent her, even hate her, so much that they'd want to terrify her—drive her away from her home

And why was Quint so certain that this demented stranger wasn't nearby? She walked the overgrown path only because he assured her she was safe here. She wanted and needed to have faith in him and his strength to protect her. But how did he know?

Most agonizing of all, what did Quint really feel for her? He told her he would take care of her. Sometimes he told her this in an almost ferocious way, as if he would defend her with everything he had. His kisses, the almost uncontrolled fever of his embraces, told her he desired her. Yet he had made it clear that he did not love her.

The path ended. Miranda, still too agitated to relax, pressed on, stepping over brambles, pushing branches clear of her way. She was amazed by the ease and silence with which Bump followed her. The river tumbled over a series of white-water rapids she hadn't seen before.

Breathing hard, she reached a small clearing. She stood for a moment, taking her bearings, looking out at the surging waters of the Flirtation.

Bump, able to stand beside her at last, reached up and gave her a wet kiss on the throat with his raspy tongue. She hugged his neck and stroked the velvety skin under his jaw. Somewhere a cardinal spilled out its liquid notes.

Then the shot rang out. Miranda heard its sharp report, and almost simultaneously a startling zing struck somewhere behind her as the bullet ricocheted off rock. Bump, his wild instincts springing to life, tensed and leaped away. Miranda stood, her heart hammering crazily, too dazed even to look after him. Then the second shot rang out, a crack of pure menace, and again the rock behind her shrieked as the bullet jolted off it.

He's come! she thought in panic. The crazed letter writer—he'd tracked her down. Quint was wrong!

Blindly terrified, Miranda fled after Bump, crashing back into the cover of the forest. She ignored the brambles and overhanging limbs that tried to block her way. With all the fleetness in her young body, she hurtled through the woods, ignoring the clutch of hanging vines, the leg-gouging traps of the briers.

Scratched, knees scraped, clothing torn, she reached the clearing and Quint's cabin at last. Chest heaving raggedly, lungs burning, she stumbled inside, barely conscious that Bump stood like an uneasy sentry beside the door or that Boots was barking madly.

She crashed into the cabin and instinctively ran to Quint's arms. She threw herself into them, clutching his waist as if she were drowning and he the only certain means of survival.

"Miranda!" He held her away from him a moment. He took in her punished body and torn clothes. But mostly he took in the terror that shone in her eyes, robbing her expression of all reason. Instinctively he knew he must hold her as tightly as he could. His arms enclosed her like protective bands of iron.

"Miranda," he repeated against her hair. "It's all right. I have you. What is it?"

She began to sob, and once she began, she could not control herself.

"Miranda," he kept saying as he rocked her in his arms. At last he picked her up and carried her into the bedroom where he laid her down on the bed. He stretched beside her taking her into the shelter of his arms again. "Hush," he said softly, rocking her again. "Hush, darlin'. Hush. I have you. I have you. You're fine."

Before he quite knew what was happening, he was kissing her tears away, trying to still the trembling of her mouth with his own lips. He smoothed her tangled hair, then he wiped clean a scratch on her cheek, then kissed the mark.

"What was it?" he whispered, holding her tight.

At last, her tears spent, feeling safe in the refuge of his arms, she managed to gasp out the story. When she stumbled in the telling, he said, "There, there," and kissed her, then urged her to go on.

"Shot at you?" he said with angry disbelief when she reached that part of the story. "*Shot* at you?"

"Twice," she panted. "He shot twice. He's here, Quint. He's really followed me here. I don't know what he'll do to me—to us."

"No," he uttered with finality. He held her close to him a moment longer. She felt his body give a long subtle shudder. Then he raised up, drawing her beside him so both of them sat on the edge of the bed. "Listen," he said, looking deep into her eyes. "It's a coincidence. That's all. You've got to believe that. You're safe with me. Safe."

"Coincidence?" she replied in disbelief, her face pale with fright.

"Coincidence," he repeated. "It must have been Slayton. Either up to something and firing a shot to warn you off—or after Bump. He's done it before—tried to frighten people off with a shot. But never on my property. But he wasn't actually after you, Miranda. You've got to believe that and get control of yourself."

"Slayton?" she cried. "After Bump? Or just trying to scare me? You can't believe that."

"I believe it and I know it," he said firmly. "Miranda, I never warned you about him, because he's never had the nerve to move into my territory before. If I catch him here, or ever catch him threatening to harm a hair of your head, he'll hate the day he was born."

"But—" she objected. Suddenly his arms no longer seemed like a sanctuary. He didn't believe her. He didn't understand the danger.

"Trust me!" he insisted, still staring into her eyes. "These damned letters have you frightened out of your skin. I'm going to stop them."

"Stop them?" she said. She resisted the urge to laugh hysterically.

"Yes," he asserted. He smoothed her hair once more, touched the mark on her face. "But I'll have to go away for a while. And leave you here."

"Leave me?" Miranda repeated aghast. "You can't leave me here alone—please! Please, Quint!"

"You won't be alone," he soothed. "I'll get Harry's boy to stay—he can camp behind the cabin. And a security man from Little Rock. Two, if it'll make you feel better. Three, if you want."

"No," she said desperately. "Please. Don't leave me." Her hands clutched at the collar of his shirt. "Please."

Gently he pried her fingers loose. "Trust me," he said again. He stood, because he knew he couldn't touch her any longer.

He looked down at her with feigned calm. "You'll be fine. I'll take care of this letter thing, then take care of Slayton when I come back. You'll be fine as long as you stick close to the cabin."

"No!" she cried. "I don't want you to leave."

"I've got to," he said softly. "Go on now. Wash your face."

"Please don't go," she begged.

But he turned and walked out the door without looking back. "I've got to" was all he said. "Tomorrow." He didn't have the heart to tell her that after he did what he had to do she might never want to see him again. And he wouldn't blame her.

She watched him walk away. She trembled in spite of herself. She wiped ineffectually at her eyes. When he walked out the bedroom door, it was as if he took all her meager security, her reason for living, with him.

But when she finally fell asleep that night, he was awake, sitting in the front room, his gun waiting in case Slayton or anyone else should dare try to harm her. Nobody was going to hurt her. Except him, he thought darkly. Except him. He was going to hurt her terribly. And he had no choice.

CHAPTER ELEVEN

QUINT LEFT the next afternoon. He was silent and his jaw had the steely set she had come to know so well. He wore a three-piece charcoal-gray suit she hadn't known he'd owned. Except for the hardness of his expression, he looked remarkably handsome. He didn't remind her of a businessman in the suit. He reminded her of a gunfighter who has donned his best in honor of the danger of his task.

True to Quint's word, the teenage Jamie McIver came to help with the animals. He would stay in a pup tent behind the cabin, and he'd brought his rifle, just in case.

The two security people Quint had hired from Little Rock also arrived. They jolted into the clearing in a large camper covered with travel stickers. They appeared shortly before Quint left and introduced themselves as Lefty and Alma Metz. Lefty was a wiry little man of deceptively mild appearance. He said he had been a deputy for twenty years. Now retired, he did security work when he and Alma weren't pursuing their sunset dreams of travel.

Alma Metz, considerably taller and heftier than her husband, seemed at first the more formidable of the two. A retired jail matron and cook, she was sufficiently large and forceful to deal with the most uncooperative adversary. But, Miranda soon found out, in spite of Alma's facade of toughness, she was actually a quiet woman whose three loves in life were Lefty, cooking and the camper.

Quint's brisk and serious orders to Jamie, Lefty and Alma showed he had inherited Duke's military efficiency

Nights, Alma was to stay in the cabin with Miranda. Lefty would stay in the camper, keeping guard out front; Jamie's post was behind the cabin. Miranda was to go nowhere alone. Under no circumstances was she to wander from the immediate area of the clearing. Everyone was to keep an eye out for evidence of Slayton. Harry McIver or the sheriff was to be called immediately if Slayton was sighted.

Quint took Miranda inside for a brief goodbye. He had steadfastly refused to tell her where he was going or what precisely he intended to do. From the stoniness of his features, she knew better than to ask again.

He struck her as both distinguished and slightly menacing. The deep tan of his angular face contrasted with the snowy white of his shirt. His dark hair, slightly too long to be fashionable, was combed back carefully from his brow.

She thought Quint's dark blue eyes softened when he stood gazing down at her. But she could not be sure. She was never sure of anything when it came to Quint.

"I don't know how long I'll be gone." His voice still had that no-nonsense military precision.

"A week?" she questioned. Her eyes seemed caught by his, and she felt hypnotized. She didn't want him to be gone for a week. She did not want him to be gone at all, and felt frightened and betrayed by his leaving.

"Shouldn't be that long," he uttered. The vein in his temple pulsed. "I—" He paused. The vein danced again. "I don't want to do what I have to," he continued. "But it's got to be done. I want you to understand."

"But I don't." Her throat tightened with confusion and unhappiness.

"You will."

"And when you come back?" She looked up at him, trying to keep some semblance of pride. Her overloaded emotions weighed on her chest like a stone.

"Then you should be free," he said gruffly.

"Free?" she asked, not liking the sound of the word at all.

"To go home," he explained matter-of-factly. "Or wherever you want."

What if I don't want to go anywhere? she wanted to cry. *What if I want to stay here with you? Forever?* She was afraid the shameless questions shone from her eyes. She looked away from Quint, stared at the floor.

"Take care of yourself," he admonished her in the same controlled voice. "Do exactly as I've told you. And call Pop while I'm gone, okay? He gets restless. He likes to hear from you. All right?"

"All right." Miranda nodded. The weight on her chest seemed heavier and heavier, as if it might crush her.

They stood for a moment in awkward silence. At last, to her perplexity, he lifted her chin so she had to look into his face again. "I'm not doing this to hurt you," he muttered. "Believe that. I'm trying to set you free. Understand?"

The touch of his fingers against her face filled her with emotions as tumultuous as the beating of giant wings. She felt almost ill with longing. Her lips trembled.

"I understand," she lied. For a dizzying moment she believed he might lower his head and kiss her with that passionate intensity that turned her into a dark and hungry flame.

But his hand fell away. He almost smiled, but did not. "Behave, okay?"

"Sure." She nodded weakly. Then he turned and left her standing alone. With surprising clarity she thought, *So this is what it feels like when somebody breaks your heart. It feels like dying.*

But Miranda had dealt with heartbreak, albeit of another sort, all her life. In fact, handling rejection was her specialty, and she wasn't about to fall to pieces now—at least not outwardly. She had perfected pretending to an art

She waited for the roar of the van's motor and the spatter of gravel beneath its wheels to tell her that Quint was gone. Then she fed the squirrels and went out to help Jamie with the other animals. She was so cheerful that nobody suspected she was the least bit unhappy. Indeed, they all probably thought that for someone needing protection from danger she was remarkably unconcerned, even a bit featherheaded.

SHE SHOULD HAVE counted on Duke, bedridden as he was, to keep things lively and on the move. When she called, he informed her he was sending his contractor to the Flirtation that afternoon. "It's time Quint built a decent house," Duke grumbled. "He can't live all his life like a hermit."

I think that's just what he wants, Miranda thought gloomily, but she said nothing.

"This bum leg has made me think harder about retiring," Duke went on in his usual thunderous tones. "If I come down to the Flirtation to fish, I don't want to sleep in one of those danged bunk beds. I want to live like an adult human being—not a Boy Scout. Besides, Quint needs better facilities to entertain board members and contributors. He never thinks of things like that. Or that he might have a family someday. He planned that house five years ago. It's time we got to it."

"Are you sure he wants it?" Miranda asked nervously. The mention of Quint having a family someday pained her, for she knew she would be no part of it. And Quint was so independent, she wondered if he would resist Duke's sudden decision to start building.

"Of course he wants it," Duke said with typical impatience. "If he'd stop to think about it he would. And he ain't 'bout to fight with his old daddy. He respects me too much. Which is altogether fittin' and proper."

"He does respect you," Miranda replied, smiling. *And he loves you,* she added silently. *Just as you love him.* How strange, she thought. Duke and Quint were so different— opposites in many ways. But they felt esteem and deep fondness for each other.

"Ah, honey," Duke said, "my boys lose patience with me sometimes, but they know I don't lie, I don't expect 'em to be nobody but themselves, and I got their best interests at heart."

"Well, bless you for that," Miranda said, getting a choking feeling in her throat. With Duke behind him, no wonder Quint had survived his nightmarish adolescence. She liked Duke better every day. Ironically, she felt more comfortable with him than her own father. He was one more reason, red-haired and frequently roaring, that she didn't want to leave.

That night, sleep eluded her. Her mind swirled. Where had Quint gone, and why? Did he really think he would find her pursuer? How could he, when the detective her father hired had discovered nothing?

Most disturbing, if he found the source of the letters, how would it affect Miranda's future? There would no longer be any need for her to stay in Quint's unwilling care. But where would she go? Switzerland, as her father wanted? Did she even care what her father wanted any longer? Once she had idolized him. Now, after comparing him to Duke, she wondered why it was so hard, so *impossible*, for her father to love her.

She had also begun to doubt that Jaqueline's concern and affection were as genuine as Jaqueline liked to pretend. Once she had admired her sister, but lately Miranda perceived that all her life Jaqueline had been playing games with her. Some had been subtle and some not so subtle, but all had delivered the same underlying message. *You, Mir anda, are not as good as we are. You don't belong in this family.*

She had known how they felt and fought all her life to belong—belong with her own family. But she'd fought in vain. She might as well have been left on their doorstep and grudgingly taken in. The question that frightened her was if she would ever belong anywhere. The first place she had truly thought she might belong was with Quint. But he was like her father and Jaqueline. He simply did not want her. The difference was that he was honest about it.

When she finally slept she dreamed she was in Quint's arms, and his mouth took hers with such abandon that he possessed not only her lips but her very soul. She awoke bereft next morning, knowing the only time she might ever taste those drugging kisses again would be in dreams.

THE CONTRACTOR, a man named Ike Beasley, showed up again the next afternoon. The previous day he and his assistant had come shortly after Quint left. Beasley found the levelest part of the mountain's slope near the emergency pens. He and his assistant roughly surveyed and staked out the best location for the building, took a series of photos of the site, then returned to Little Rock to consult Duke.

Beasley had said he'd return to survey the site more precisely and take the elevations. But he came in a bad mood, for his regular assistant had the flu, and his part-time assistant had broken his foot in a motorcycle accident, and Beasley himself had an incipient case of poison ivy from walking the woods the day before.

Lefty offered to help Beasley with the surveying tapes and rods. Alma was in the cabin cooking lunch, for Lefty was on a special diet and Alma trusted no one else to minister to his dietary needs. Jamie McIver got careless cleaning the raccoons' cage and was bitten. His finger bleeding profusely, he stalked, grumbling, back to the cabin.

Miranda, alone at the emergency pens, finished changing the foxes' water. She could hear Beasley and Lefty farther down the slope. The thought of the lovely house being started when she was soon to leave saddened her.

Behind her usual facade of cheerfulness she had spent the morning brooding. Suddenly an alarming thought pierced the fog of her moodiness—she hadn't seen Bump all day. She had been too lost in her own thoughts to miss him. Now his absence struck her, filling her with apprehension.

She called him. She heard nothing except the wind in the leaves. Again she called. Bump did not appear.

Miranda looked around nervously. The young buck could have gone anywhere, but one of his favorite jaunts seemed to be along the river. Still calling his name, she descended the slope.

She passed the cabin and saw Alma steering a reluctant Jamie toward the camper. "Where you goin', girl?" Alma called to her.

"I'm looking for the tame deer," Miranda said, brushing a long curl away from her forehead. "Where are *you* going?"

"I'm goin' to have to take Jamie to town to the doctor. That coon has done bit his finger to the bone," Alma said, practically forcing Jamie into the cab of the camper. "Don't you go wanderin' off, hear? You wait for Lefty. And tell him I put the egg salad in the refrigerator."

Miranda nodded mechanically and watched them drive off. She hoped Jamie wasn't injured seriously. The raccoons had been inoculated against disease, but they could still inflict a wicked bite.

She looked down the narrow path along the river's edge and called Bump. Again there was no response.

"Drat," muttered Miranda, deciding she should follow the path a short way at least. Bump often went exploring on his own but seldom for long.

She called Boots, but he didn't appear. He must be with Beasley and Lefty up the mountainside. She didn't relish the idea of following the path alone, but at least it was in the opposite direction from where the shot had rung out the other day.

This path, less traveled than the other, was more choked with vines, more blocked by overhanging limbs. Miranda moved as quickly as she could, but the constant curving of the track and the thickness of the underbrush confused her sense of progress. She was not sure how far she had come or how long it had taken her.

The woods were eerily quiet. She suddenly remembered all too clearly her terror of two days before and decided to turn back. It was then that she saw them—deer tracks, clear and fresh in the soft earth. The hoofprints might have been only minutes old. They led farther down river. Bump had apparently picked his way through the woods, stepped onto the path at this point, then continued south.

Softly she called his name. All she heard in reply was the lapping of the river, which was slow at this point. "Drat," she said again. She wanted to return to the safety of the clearing—but she wanted to find Bump. From the look of his tracks, he might be only minutes away. She gritted her teeth in determination, then tried to make her way more quietly along the path.

Suddenly she heard a quick, almost frantic burst of rustling ahead of her around a bend in the path. "Bump?" Her voice was almost a whisper.

Another brief flurry of rustles answered her, along with a strange, muted noise like none she had ever heard. Swallowing hard, she pushed the branches out of her way and hurried onward. The low, strangled moan sounded again.

She rounded the bend, then stopped in uncomprehending shock. Bump seemed to be kneeling before her at the side of the path, his front legs buckled to the earth, his rear in the air, his hind legs tensed and straining. His head was near the ground, his beautiful eyes rolling wildly.

"Bump!" she breathed in horror. He tried to raise his head. He kicked out helplessly with one taut hind leg. He was helpless, his sleek neck caught tightly in a snare. He was choking himself to death with useless struggling.

"Bump!" Miranda cried again, sinking to her knees beside him. *Slayton,* she thought in panic and fury. *Quint had been right.* Slayton wanted Bump. He must have seen the old hoofprints on the path and set the snare.

Bump thrashed more wildly when she tried to help him. Perhaps he thought Miranda's mere presence should magically free him and that he could spring away. Throwing one arm around his tortured neck, she tried to calm him, while her right hand tugged at the knot of the noose that imprisoned him. She cursed herself for not carrying a jackknife.

Bump fought so hard to be free that she could barely get hold of the knot. His panicky resistance pulled the noose tighter still. Miranda bit her lip. Tears smeared her vision. He was going to kill himself before her very eyes.

"Bump! Please!" she pleaded. "Please!"

His struggles only increased. Then his back legs kicked spasmodically and collapsed, and with a piteous sound almost like a croak, he fell heavily to his side. He lay still.

"Oh, please, Bump," Miranda prayed, her fingers clumsy against the complicated knot. "Please!" Either he'd cut off his wind completely and was dying, she thought, or he'd broken his slender neck and was dead already.

Sobbing, her nails torn, she finally managed to release him from the imprisoning rope. He gasped raggedly. He began to breathe. His eyes half opened, but he lay in a daze, panting brokenly. Miranda collapsed, still weeping, against the smoothness of his shoulder, one hand running over his punished neck. "Please get up," she begged him. "Please be all right. Please get well."

Then there was a rattle in the brush before her, and a strange voice spoke. "Set out to catch me one pretty little deer. Looks like I done caught two."

The words, the harshness of the voice, chilled her flesh, made her stomach leap with fright. She raised her smudged face, her eyes wide with foreboding.

A dirty-looking man of medium height stood before her, a rifle held loosely in his hands but aimed in her direction. He wore a tattered shirt and pants in camouflage colors, mud-spattered work boots and a brown billed cap shadowing his gaunt face.

"Two pretty little deer," he said. "One to butcher—" he glanced down briefly at Bump, who was still dazed and panting "—and one to play with." The pale blue eyes shone maliciously out of his unshaven face as he looked at Miranda again. He grinned at her. Two of his front teeth were gone.

She sat up. Panic flooded through her, but mixed with it was rage, and rage, she sensed, might be exactly what she needed to survive.

"Mr. Slayton," she said, her voice shaking. "The intrepid poacher, I take it."

"Don't talk smart," he warned. "Don't talk at all. I seen you afore. The other day. Pretty girl like you shouldn't be out in the woods alone. To my mind, that makes you fair game." He grinned again.

His implication was clear and made Miranda feel sick to her stomach. She glared up at him, but her chin trembled. She had an absurd flash of memory. She had sometimes felt almost this frightened in Cambasia when she had tried to slip away and Duke had surprised her, springing on her with one of his bloodcurdling battle cries. He always terrified her, and the fact he had terrified enraged her. She had fought his carrying her off more than once—until it took most of

Duke's skill and all of his patience to get them both back
unscathed.

"And I'll decide exactly what games we's gonna play,"
Slayton smirked, "as soon as I put your friend here out of
his misery."

He turned Bump's head up slightly with the toe of his
work boot. *No!* Miranda thought wildly as he brought the
rifle to the deer's skull. *No! Fight!*

She flung herself across Bump's body as hard as she
could. With both hands she wrested the rifle barrel away
from its target. Somehow she had rolled completely over
Bump, and she kicked at Slayton's legs with all her might.
She pulled harder still on the rifle barrel. The suddenness of
her attack surprised him, allowing her to jerk the barrel
down hard enough to jam it into the soft earth. He was a
strong man and fought to snatch it away. But Miranda had
the strength of desperation and managed to hang on. And
she kept kicking, hard enough to make Slayton yelp with
pain.

The noise and confusion shook Bump out of his daze.
Awkwardly he scrambled to his feet and leaped away, back
toward the cabin.

Slayton swore and tried to raise the rifle again to take aim
at the fleeing deer, but Miranda kept her hold a few seconds longer. When he finally wrenched the barrel from her
grasp, it was too late. Bump was gone.

Miranda started to scramble after him, her surge of brav-
ery vanishing. But suddenly the rifle barrel was trained on
her once more, and Slayton stood above her, his bony face
rigid with resentment. This time she knew it would be sheer
folly to snatch at the gun.

He loomed over her. He looked down the rifle sight at her
pale face. "You made me lose that deer," he said in a voice
as menacing as a snake's hiss. "And you kicked at me.
You're gonna pay. I know how to take the hell out of a hell-

cat. I know all kinds of ways. Ways you're gonna wish you never learnt."

"Touch me," Miranda said with false bravado, "and you'll have the FBI and the Secret Service to deal with. My father's very high in the government. They'll lock you up and throw away the key."

"You don't scare me," he mocked, the gap-toothed grin slicing his face.

"How about me?" asked a deceptively calm voice behind him. "Do I scare you, Slayton? I should. Because I'd gladly kill."

Slayton whirled, trying to aim his rifle in the direction of the voice behind him. But he was too late. Quint's own rifle struck Slayton's from his hands. It spun away into the bush.

"Wilcox!" Slayton's voice was disbelieving.

"Here with a news bulletin," Quint said in his coldest voice. "Hunting season's over." His rifle butt flashed out and connected with the point of Slayton's grizzled chin. The poacher swayed a second, looking suddenly boneless in his dirty clothing. He pitched to the ground like a felled tree.

Then Quint's arms were about Miranda, pulling her to her feet. Even though he was none too gentle, she collapsed against him gratefully.

"Are you all right?" His tone was strained.

"I'm fine—just scared. Thank God you came. How did you find us?" she asked, burying her face against his broad chest.

"I met Alma and Jamie on the lane, getting ready to turn onto the road. Jamie said you were worried about Bump. When I couldn't find you, I put two and two together, saw your tracks on the south path, grabbed my Winchester and came after you. Didn't I warn you not to go off alone?"

He held her away from him when he said the last words and gave her a slight shake. She felt giddy, light-headed to the point of faintness. His hair hung in his eyes. Burrs clung to his suit coat. His tie was loose and his collar slightly torn.

"Oh," she said irrelevantly, "you came clear through the woods in your nice suit—I hope it isn't ruined."

He shook his head hopelessly. He folded her in his arms again. "Miranda," he sighed harshly. "You're more trouble than any woman I ever met." But he kept holding her. For the moment it was enough.

Then he held her away from him again and studied her face. It was tearstained, smudged with dirt and far too pale. It was also, he thought, the most beautiful face he'd ever seen. But soon it was going to register more pain, the worst kind of pain, and he would be responsible for inflicting it.

"Come on," he muttered. "I'm going to truss this piece of slime up in his own rope, then call Harry to take him away and keep him away. Then I want to make sure you're all right. And then we've got to talk. All of us."

"All of us?" she asked, puzzled. She wondered why he looked so grim. His face seemed to hold more complex emotions than mere anger at her disobedience.

"You and I and Buford," Quint said, his expression not changing. "Buford's here."

"Buford?" Miranda cried. "Here?"

"Miranda—" His eyes looked regretful, almost pitying. "We've got things to tell you that aren't good. Not good at all. I brought Buford back so he can take you to Switzerland—or wherever you want to go."

No! Miranda thought in anguished protest. *What was happening to her now?* She wanted to cry, as she had done for Bump, but she held her tears in check.

Looking at her stricken face, Quint felt a shaft of guilt go through him. "You're sure you're all right?" he asked. "Slayton scared you more than hurt you?"

Miranda shrugged nonchalantly, although she still felt shaky. "Surface wounds," she said, trying unsuccessfully to sound composed. "I'll be healed in a week. I'm a survivor."

"Yes," he said tonelessly. "You are." He couldn't tell her yet that her biggest test was coming. But he didn't want to think about it. He concentrated on getting her back to the cabin so he could call Harry.

MIRANDA MOVED in a daze for the rest of the afternoon. She had flown into Buford's arms, and he had comforted her, obviously upset by her confrontation with Slayton. But otherwise he was strangely restrained. Obviously he didn't want to talk until the business with Slayton was taken care of and the other people left the compound. After the initial warmth of his greeting, he seemed troubled and distracted, not at all the usually self-confident man Miranda knew. Most disturbing, he refused to reveal why he was there. "Later" was all he'd say. "We'll talk later."

Miranda nodded numbly. Buford's presence seemed pleasant but unreal, like something occurring in a dream. The whole episode with Slayton struck her as equally unreal, as if it had taken place in a recent nightmare. In the meantime, too much else was happening. Miranda felt groggy, unsure she'd ever be able to focus her attention again.

She begged Quint to examine Bump, who stood trembling in the clearing, his legs still shaking. Quint complied. But as his sure fingers moved over Bump's neck and chest, he was bombarding Lefty and Beasley, the contractor, with questions. What in blazes was Beasley doing there, and why in blazes was Lefty helping him instead of watching Miranda, as he'd been paid to do? Beasley sputtered, Lefty stuttered, and Miranda, shaken and guilty, insisted on taking all the blame.

"No use taking it out on them," Buford told Quint at last. He had stood quietly, watching the whole tense exchange. "Takes a better man than ordinary to keep Miranda out of trouble. If you don't believe me, ask your daddy."

Miranda, on her knees beside Bump, flashed him a look that was half grateful and half guilty. Quint regarded Buford in silence a moment, then nodded. Beasley and Lefty looked relieved, even though they seemed a bit insulted at being called "ordinary" men.

The confusion was heightened by the arrival of two sheriff's deputies, followed by Harry McIver in his truck. They had come for the bruised and bound Slayton. After delivering Miranda safely back to the clearing, Quint had retrieved Slayton, lugging him over his shoulder like a side of beef. Slayton was still only semiconscious, and one of the deputies expressed concern that Quint had given the poacher a concussion.

"I don't care if I knocked his head off," Quint returned coldly. "He was tryin' to hurt the girl."

Harry McIver, who had seemed more concerned with Miranda's safety than Slayton's capture, gave Quint a sharp look. A light of understanding dawned on his broad face. He glanced at Miranda, then at Quint, then at Miranda again. He obviously realized Miranda and Quint were not cousins; they had simply been living together. He blushed. Miranda blushed herself, for Harry was a kind man and they had lied to him. She would write him a letter of apology as soon as she was gone.

The deputies hauled Slayton away, and Harry, still looking wounded, followed. Then Alma appeared with a bandaged Jamie in tow, and explanations and questions and exclamations and confusion all arose again. Miranda tried to stay silent and kept by Bump, her arms around his neck. He butted his head against her shoulder repeatedly, as if assuring himself she were real.

Finally Quint dismissed Lefty and Alma, sending them on their way. He was polite, but Miranda could tell he was angry with them for letting her slip away. He apologized brusquely to Beasley, told him to get on with the plans but that this was obviously not the time to talk about them. To Jamie he was kinder, but it was obvious to all that Quint's patience was at its end: he wanted to be alone with Miranda and Buford.

Jamie was the last to leave, his bandaged hand crooked awkwardly on the handlebar of his motorcycle. He roared off down the lane, and Miranda, still clinging to Bump, watched him go.

"You shouldn't have been so hard on Lefty and Alma," she said, not looking at Quint. "It was my fault."

"I hired them to watch you," he said shortly. "They didn't."

"All's well that ends well," Buford put in, eyeing them both. "Unless, of course, folks want to go on arguing about it until we all fall down dead with boredom."

Miranda rose and turned to Buford. "Now that everybody's gone, are you going to stop being so mysterious? What are you doing here?"

Buford's dark face was suddenly unreadable. "I've come to take you to Switzerland—or wherever it is you want to go. And then I'm going to Saint Louis."

Miranda tried to ignore the sick, sinking feeling that filled her. Quint watched her, his face even stonier than Buford's.

"I don't want to go to Switzerland," she protested weakly. "And why are you going to Saint Louis?"

"Because I'm going home," Buford said with quiet dignity. "I've quit. I don't work for the Senator anymore."

"Buford!" Her gray-green eyes widened in shock. Home without Buford was unthinkable. It was no longer home at all. "How could you quit?"

"It was time. I was old enough to retire a year ago, Miranda." He shook his head sadly. "And—well, honey, I had enough."

"Enough?" she asked helplessly. She released Bump. She went to Buford and stood before him. "You're really leaving us, Buford?" She felt close to tears. She wondered if it were for the hundredth time that day.

"No," he replied stolidly. "I've stayed on these last years partly for you. But now I'm leaving *them*, Miranda. If you're smart, you'll leave them yourself. I've stood by too long watching what they tried to do. This last one was too much. I should have known. I just couldn't admit it was as bad as it was."

"What was too much? What was so bad?" She looked at Buford's shuttered expression, then at Quint, then back to Buford. "I don't understand."

Buford took her hands in his and held them very tightly. "Miranda," he said carefully. "Listen. Try to understand." There was a long pause. "Jaqueline wrote those letters. She's been sick with jealousy for years. Years, honey."

Miranda felt as if she were falling into a dark chasm. Her knees went weak. "Jaqueline?" She felt herself sinking slowly toward the ground.

Quint's hands grasped her, supported her. "Steady," he ordered harshly in her ear. He guided her to the old wicker rocker that sat before the cabin. Buford kept hold of her hands. Buford's touch comforted her, but Quint's, while it kept her erect, somehow made her hurt all the more.

As soon as she sat, Quint released her, but she could feel his presence close behind her. Buford knelt before her, gripping her hands more tightly than before.

"She's been jealous of you since you were little—everybody in the house knew how she loved to tattle on you." Buford watched her face carefully. "The older you got, the worse it got. She wanted to be the one everyone admired. She was jealous of everything—even your father's attention when he was mad at you. And I think she was scared to death you'd take her new boyfriend. She wanted to keep you away.''

"Jealous?" Miranda felt torn between laughter and tears. "Of me? I never wanted her boyfriends—ever!"

"That didn't matter," Buford said patiently. "What mattered was she was afraid they'd want *you*. Didn't you ever notice if she even thought one of her beaux looked at you, she was through with him? She was scared of what would happen if Delbert saw you. So scared it twisted her.''

"But I've always been jealous of Jaqueline," Miranda cried. "I tried not to be, but I was. How could she be jealous of me? She was perfect.''

"What she was perfect at was imitating your daddy," Buford explained. "But you were the one with the warmth—and the fire. You were the one people noticed. You were the one with *life*.''

"But everyone admired her—and Daddy always said she was perfect," Miranda objected, trying to hold back her tears.

"Miranda," Buford said sadly, "everybody admired a few things about Jaqueline. Only your daddy thought she was perfect. Because she was just like him.''

"But those letters—how could she write those awful letters?" Miranda withdrew her hands from Buford's and hid her face in them.

"I told you," Buford said, patting her knee inadequately. "She liked this young man so much and was so jealous, she just went a little crazy.''

"Did she admit it?" Miranda's voice was muffled. "How did you guess she wrote them?"

"She admitted it," Buford replied grimly. "Quinton figured it out. I should have. I guess I didn't want to. Me, with all my psychology. I didn't want it to be true. I just wanted to get you down here with Duke where you'd be safe.''

Quint did not touch her. His voice was husky with control. ''I knew something was wrong that day I took you to the doctor, Miranda, when you told me you still had the letters. If your father had any kind of decent detective, the letters should have been turned over to him. They were clues—evidence—but nobody'd ever asked you for them. It made no sense.''

It made no sense at all, Miranda thought numbly, unless her father hadn't wanted to catch the culprit at all. And that meant he had suspected all along it was Jaqueline—and had protected her at Miranda's expense. No wonder Buford had quit in disgust. And how Quint must disdain them all, including her.

Miranda began to cry softly. Buford rose to stand awkwardly beside her. It was his arm, not Quint's, that went around her in affectionate protection.

Quint's voice went on, cool with detachment. ''The postmarks were misleading. Lots of businesses exist merely for the purpose of mailing other people's letters—no question asked. The writer could have been in Washington the whole time. When I saw the letters, I knew something was wrong. The threats were vague. Men don't usually make threats like that—women do. Finally, the misspellings were strange—inconsistent—obviously somebody pretending to be less than literate.''

Miranda's head throbbed. Somebody who probably lived in Washington. Someone who was a woman. Someone who was bright but pretending to be stupid. Someone whom her father wanted to protect. Quint had deduced it with no problem at all—someone who could only be Jaqueline.

Buford handed her his beautifully folded handkerchief. He patted her shoulder and let her cry.

"Daddy had to know," she said at last, her face still hidden in her hands. "He had to guess. How could he let her do it?"

"Your daddy was frightened, Miranda. And angry. Same way he's been most of his life. He tried to make himself believe Jaqueline would get over it as soon as she was married—that the whole escapade was your fault, not hers. That you'd brought it on yourself."

Miranda looked up at him. "But why?" she demanded. How far could her father's mad favoritism go? "How could he let her do it to me? I'm his daughter, too!"

Her pained eyes held Buford's dark ones. He stared at her gently. He went down on one knee beside her again. He took her left hand between both of his. His lips said nothing, but the pain in his eyes told her something she had always secretly feared.

"You've had enough shocks for one day, honey," he said. He patted her hand. "Let's go inside. Let's get some food in you."

She shook her head. Suddenly everything seemed very clear, logical and inevitable. There was no puzzle at all about why her family didn't love her.

Her eyes brimmed with tears, but a sudden brave stubbornness leaped in them, too. Her gaze never wavered from Buford's. "I'm not, am I?" she asked softly. "I'm not his daughter at all. Tell the truth, Buford. I think maybe I've always felt it, even if I never knew it. I just never fit in. Ever."

Buford was silent a long time. He studied the stern control with which she held herself, how she willed her tears not to fall. He decided she could take it. She was, after all, Miranda. "You're not his daughter," he affirmed solemnly. "Your father's a cold man, an insecure man. Only power makes him happy. Jaqueline's just like him. Your mother needed more. She told him so, but he wouldn't let her go. She met an officer in Cambasia—an attaché to a military adviser. His name was Captain Hap Shannon—United States Air Force. He was your father. He never knew. But he would have loved you, Miranda. You're a lot like him. Full of fire and fun."

She swallowed hard. "He was my father? He never knew?" But she sat as straight as a princess.

"The Senator suspected what was happening. He pulled strings, got Hap Shannon shipped out of Cambasia and into Laos. Hap died a few weeks later in a copter crash. Then your mother found out you were on the way, and she said she'd stay with the Senator only if he accepted you as his own. Try not to hate the Senator, honey. Every time he saw you it was like a slap in the face. Pride is all that man's got and all he's ever had."

How odd, Miranda thought dispassionately. With a few words Buford had changed not only her history but all that she had thought it had meant.

"Did he—the Senator—*want* my mother to die?" she asked, trying to swallow down a rising bitterness.

"Heavens, no!" Buford retorted, squeezing her hand until it hurt. "If he ever loved anyone, he loved your mama—in his way. It was like he lost her twice—when he drove her into Hap Shannon's arms, and then again when she died. He didn't want you, child, and that's the sad truth, but your mama said she wouldn't stay unless she had you. She just wasn't as strong as she thought."

Miranda bit her lip, made her spine stiffer yet. "Did Jaqueline know?"

"She found out," Buford nodded. "Your father told her last year. On your twenty-first birthday. Right before she met Delbert. Maybe that's what drove her to such meanness. To have been so jealous all these years, and then find she wasn't even your full sister. She twisted it in her head to where she thought you stole her mother from her.

nd half her father's attention. She was getting even. She
asn't going to share anything anymore.''

"Did Quint know?" she asked. Quint had disappeared.
he hadn't seen him go, but she knew he had left. She could
el it from the emptiness in her heart. "Did Duke know
out my real father and tell him?''

Buford shook his head. "Quint guessed Jaqueline was
nding the letters. He demanded that she and the Senator
eet him—flat *demanded* it. He insisted I be there—he said
 wanted a witness. And he kept confronting them with
hat he knew until Jaqueline finally broke down and told
m everything—including that you weren't her full sister.
uint didn't know that, Miranda. I don't think he would
ve gone after the truth so hard if he had. I never really
ew it myself. There had been rumors. To tell the truth, I
d wondered. But I wasn't certain myself until last night.''

Miranda stared down at her hand locked between Bu-
rd's strong dark ones. "What's going to happen to us all,
ford?" she asked at last.

He shook his head again. "Me, I'm going home, like I
d. But my door will always be open to you. Remember
t. Jaqueline, she'll be all right, I think. She took to her
d, but that man of hers loves her true, whether she be-
ves it or not. He's a good man, Miranda. He'll stand by
, and he'll see she gets the help she needs. 'Cause truth to
, she's more sick than evil.''

'And Daddy—'' She stopped, still feeling the odd mix-
e of numbness, emptiness and bitterness. "I mean, the
ator?''

Buford released her hand, rose, shoved his hands into his
ckets and stared out toward the river. "He won't ever
nge, Miranda. When Quint came, it turned the whole
se upside down. But all the Senator could think about
 that his reputation might be hurt. He told me to tell you
l send you to Switzerland or wherever you want to go,

and he'll support you until you're twenty-five. But he wants
you to stay away from Jaqueline for a while. Until she's
better. And he says if you don't behave, he'll cut you off.
See, he's got a reason to now. He can always tell folks you
ran off and lived with Quint Wilcox. I guess that's why he
let you stay on this river. It gave him an excuse, if he ever
wanted one, to keep you away for good."

At Miranda's surprised and resentful gasp, Buford only
sighed. "I told you, he won't change, Miranda. He can't
help it. I swear, he's more to be pitied than anything. But
I've pitied him long enough. You're going to have to learn
how to do it and take over for me. You're old enough to
understand now."

She sat still, so many emotions tumbling violently within
her that she couldn't feel any of them clearly.

"What did Quint say about all this?" she asked at last,
for no matter how shocking Buford's explanations were, it
was always Quint to whom her aching mind returned. It was
as if only he could offer safe harbor.

"He said he was sorry."

Well, Miranda demanded of herself, *what else could he
say? He was a man of few words and those two, "I'm
sorry," said it all. Who wouldn't be sorry—to be involved
in such a tangled mess and with the sort of people who could
create it?*

"Oh," she said at last.

"Miranda," Buford said awkwardly, "if you don't want
to go to Switzerland, you can always come to Saint Lou
with me awhile. I'm going to stay with my sister and her
husband at first. I know you'll want to know about your
father—your real one. You'll want to talk about him. As I
said, my door is always open."

She stood up weakly. She reached out and squeezed his
elbow. "Thanks, Buford," she whispered. "I appreciate

guess right now maybe I need to be alone for a while. I've ot a lot to think over.''

"You be all right?" he asked, concern furrowing his row.

"Of course," she tried to smile. "You know me. Noth- g's ever kept me down long."

"This isn't an ordinary setback," he objected mildly.

"Maybe it's what my whole life has been preparing me to xpect," she said softly. "Because somehow it feels as if I nally know who I am. I don't have to wonder any longer."

"You sure?"

"I'm sure."

He nodded and went into the cabin. Miranda called for ump, who had been sleeping in nervous exhaustion under mock orange bush. He sprang to his feet and followed her, uzzling her shirt affectionately as she walked down the orth river path, away from the place where she'd encoun- red Slayton.

At a place where the path descended into a small valley, e stopped and sat on a lichen-covered log. Bump stayed xt to her, laying his head in her lap, rubbing his velvety eek against her thigh. She petted him absently. She didn't ant to think about him. How was she going to leave him, her, she thought, strange, loving creature that he was? Or atso or Albert or the squirrels, for that matter?

She sat, trying to sort out her confused emotions. She was t conscious of how many hours passed. When at last the n began to sink, coloring the sky a mixture of peach and quoise, she still didn't move. She sat, stroking Bump, ring out at the darkening river. She wondered, absurdly, a woman had ever shown up in Switzerland with an ac- mpanying deer....

She heard a stick crack behind her and whirled. Part of fatalistically expected to see Slayton, somehow broken e, ready to spring on her. But a deeper, more desperate

part of her was even more terrified to see that it was Quint
She had hoped all along he would come to her. But if he did
she had no idea what he would say. Would he ask her, po
litely, to leave as soon as possible?

He stood before her. He looked his old self, his long leg
encased in tight-fitting faded jeans, his dark T-shirt, hi
Stetson pulled down over his eyes.

"You all right?" he asked, his voice toneless.

She shrugged. "I'm fine. I'm just getting used to it, that'
all."

"I suppose it's pretty strange," he commented. He pulle
his hat brim down further so she couldn't see his eyes for th
shadow.

"It's not strange," she returned. "I think I've bee
expecting it for years. It's sort of like what you said—I'm s
free."

"Miranda," he muttered, his voice gravelly, "I'm so
ry—"

"Don't be," she said crisply. "It had to happen. It ju
didn't pick the best day to happen, that's all. I start the da
by being attacked by a poacher and end it learning I'm ill
gitimate. The timing could have been better."

"I'm sorry," he continued, shifting his weight. "If I
known everything, I wouldn't have gone—"

"I said it's all right." She raised her head and tried to loo
unconcerned. She might not be the Senator's real daught
but some of his pride had rubbed off on her. Her voice w
sharper than she'd intended.

"I suppose you hate me." He sighed roughly. "Isn't th
how it works? You hate the messenger of bad news as mu
as the news. All I can say is I didn't know it would be t
bad. I'm sorry."

"Stop apologizing," Miranda ordered abruptly. "It's
your problem. And I'm not your problem any longer. Do

waste your regrets. I'll get along without them. And without you. Thanks for the memories—all of them.''

"Damn, Miranda," he growled, "if you're hurt or angry, just say so, will you?"

"I'm not hurt," she insisted. "I'm not angry, and I don't want your pity, so stop offering it."

"I'm not offering pity," he snapped back. "I'm concerned. What are you going to do now? What do you want to do?"

She looked up at him. She felt a sudden flash of anger because she cared so much and he so little. "Do? I suppose I'll go to Switzerland and find me a rich husband," she retorted. "That's one of the few options open, isn't it? I don't think I'll have any trouble. Men usually like me. They usually like me more than I find comfortable. I imagine I can find one I like back."

He swore. "Miranda," he warned, "don't talk like that." His shoulders shifted dangerously, as if he were about to enter a fray.

"I'll talk any way I want. I'm facing reality. I'm sure there are some wonderful men in Switzerland, quite attractive really, men any woman would be glad—"

"Miranda!" Quint exploded, cutting her off. He swore and tore off his Stetson, threw it to the ground. The motion startled Bump so much that he leaped away and disappeared among the cedar trees. "I said don't talk like that!" he thundered.

Miranda, too worn by the day's events, rose rebelliously, tossing her hair. "Why not?" she demanded. "What business is it of yours? You don't—"

He seized hold of her suddenly, bringing her against his chest so tightly that it hurt her. He stared fiercely down into her eyes. The vein in his temple jumped, and his nostrils flared. "You don't talk that way because I want you," he commanded roughly. His face bore down on hers and he kissed her with a ferocity of possession. After a long moment the touch of his lips gentled against hers, coaxing them, teasing them. Then his kiss became almost savage again in its intensity.

He drew back from her, breathing hard. "And you don't talk that way because I love you," he ordered. His mouth met hers again in that peculiar combination of punishment and pleasure. His fingers imprisoned her shoulders so she could not escape. He pulled away once more, his breath even more ragged.

"You don't talk that way because the only man you're ever going to have is me, Miranda. And that's that." His mouth swooped to take hers yet another time, and the primitive demand of his embrace thrilled and frightened her. She stopped resisting, gave herself up to him completely. She no longer felt capable of supporting her own weight. It was the strength of his arms that held her. A small whimper escaped her.

He stopped, staring down at her, his dark blue eyes stunned. "Miranda?" he asked, one rough hand touching her cheek. "Miranda—have I hurt you again? I didn't mean to—I shouldn't have done this." He shook his head in despair and swore again. "After all you've been through today," he said between gritted teeth. "And when I don't even know if you forgive me or can forgive me—and now I do this to you. All of a sudden I feel like Slayton. I wasn't going to tell you I loved you unless I thought you wanted to hear it. I'm sorry, Miranda, for all that's happened. But if it' any comfort, I love you. Whether you want it or not. And don't want you to go."

"Yes," Miranda said helplessly, putting her hands on hi shoulders, touching the strong, bronzed pillar of his throat.

"Yes what?" he asked passionately, holding her mor tightly and bringing his face nearer hers.

"Yes, I love you," she admitted, closing her eyes, for the sight of him made her faint with yearning. "And yes, I want you to love me. I've wanted it forever. And yes, I want to stay with you."

He said her name again and kissed her. Between kisses, he kept uttering one word against her lips. *Love.* She answered his questing lips with her own, felt his hands moving over her with the slow, savoring pleasure of discovery.

At last he pulled back slightly, laughed softly. "How did I ever end up wanting you this much, when I started off not wanting you at all?"

"I don't know," she whispered, laying her head against his chest.

"I do," he murmured, gathering a handful of her golden hair and speaking against her throat. "I love you because you're perfect."

"Not me," she sighed happily, shaking her head. "I've never been perfect."

He took her face between his hands, stared down at her intently. "Perfect for me, Miranda," he breathed. "In every way. As if all our strengths and weaknesses were designed to compensate each other's. As if someone planned that we should be together. I didn't want to admit it." Quint shook his head and grinned down at her as if he were slightly dazed. "I guess because I'd been alone for so long, Miranda, I'd made up my mind that's the way I wanted to be forever. Then you came along. And I realized I wanted to join the human race again—that a man alone isn't complete. And never will be. You make me whole, Miranda."

"I didn't think you'd ever care for me at all," Miranda said, still tasting the wonder of it.

"I fought it," he conceded, then kissed her chin and the tip of her nose. "But in the past twenty-four hours—ever since Jaqueline broke down, it's been like one thing after another has been telling me what a fool I'd be to let you go—knowing how brave and defiant and full of spirit you've been all your life—knowing you might never forgive me. Seeing Slayton trying to hurt you. I came within an inch of killing him, I swear. But how could I tell you then? When there was so much more for you to go through—when there still is."

"I can go through it if you're with me," she said, and kissed the harsh curve of his jaw.

"Miranda, if you'll have me and the crazy life I offer, I'll go through all of life with you. And I'll love you to the last drop of my heart's blood. I promise. Marry me. Marry me as soon as they get the new house built."

He kissed her again. "No," she said, her lips brushing his. "Sooner."

"Sooner it is," he sighed deeply. "This is wonderful, Miranda. Do you suppose they knew—Buford and my father—this would happen if you came down here?"

She went suddenly still in his arms. She blinked up at him in surprise. Duke and his quiet, solitary son. Buford and his anything-but-quiet charge, Miranda. Buford, all her life, taking care of her and outsmarting her at the same time; Buford, ever affectionate and ever scheming. And Duke, who had never forgotten her and welcomed her as if she'd always belonged.

"You know," she breathed, shaking her head in delighted bewilderment, "somehow—and I don't know how—I think they did know. Does it make you feel manipulated?"

"No," he smiled. "It just proves one thing. Know what?"

"No." She beamed up at him, lips parted, waiting for his kiss. "What?"

"That we're very lucky," he told her. "Because somebody loves us both very much."

He kissed her in such a way that she knew that they would say no more with words for a long time. Their bodies and

their desires would speak instead, with long-pent eloqu-
ence.

BACK IN FRONT of the cabin, Buford sat in the wicker rocking chair looking up at the rising moon and then down at
Boots. The dog sat unhappily, chained to a post in the yard.
Bump, sulky at being ignored, lay beside the collie. Buford
rose from the rocker and stretched.

The dog, too, got up and looked into the woods, whining
and wagging its tail hopefully. Bump pricked his ears and
stared in the same direction.

"Boys," Buford said with a weary but pleased yawn,
"I'm going to bed. If you're smart, you will, too. Ain't no
sense in the world waiting up for those two. No sense at all.
You'll be waiting all night long."

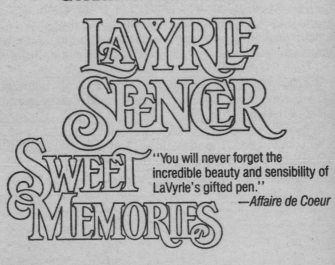

ATTRACTIVE, SPACE SAVING BOOK RACK

Display your most prized novels on this handsome and sturdy book rack. The hand-rubbed walnut finish will blend into your library decor with quiet elegance, providing a practical organizer for your favorite hard-or soft-covered books.

Only $9.95

Approximately 16" x 8" when assembled

Assembles in seconds!

To order, rush your name, address and zip code, along with a check or money order for $10.70* ($9.95 plus 75¢ postage and handling) payable to *Harlequin Reader Service*:

Harlequin Reader Service
Book Rack Offer
901 Fuhrmann Blvd.
P.O. Box 1396
Buffalo, NY 14269-1396

Offer not available in Canada.

BKR-1A

*New York and Iowa residents add appropriate sales tax.

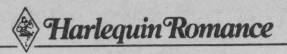
Harlequin Romance

Coming Next Month

Available in July wherever paperback books are sold, or through Harlequin Reader Service:

In the U.S.
901 Fuhrmann Blvd.
P.O. Box 1397
Buffalo, N.Y. 14240-1397

In Canada
P.O. Box 603
Fort Erie, Ontario
L2A 5X3